Now, I have to admit, being a model sounds like a pretty cool job. Flying to all parts of the world to have my picture taken, hanging out with stars, never going to school, making lots and lots of money . . . that would be great. I imagined myself on a beach with Theo Christmas, posing for a Celeb Eye magazine cover shoot. "Closer," the photographer would direct. "Theo, pull her closer." I'd rest my head against his chest and smile hugely for the camera.

And then my imagination showed me nestling with him in my polka-dot one-piece, the one with the "modesty skirt" Grandma got me to hide what she calls my "peasant" shape. Modeling might be fun, or a great opportunity, but being the face of a clothing line for chunky girls was not the type of modeling that would generate seaside celebrity photo sessions. Excessive junior high teasing? Probably. Snuggles with Theo Christmas? No way. Also, husky or not, models don't eat chocolate cookies.

Models don't eat chocolate COOKIES

by Erin Dionne

Dial Books for Young Readers

DIAL BOOKS FOR YOUNG READERS
A division of Penguin Young Readers Group • Published by The Penguin Group
Penguin Group (USA) Inc., 375 Hudson Street, New York, NY 10014, U.S.A. • Penguin Group (Canada), 90 Eglinton Avenue East, Suite 700, Toronto, Ontario, Canada
M4P 2Y3 (a division of Pearson Penguin Canada Inc.) • Penguin Books Ltd, 80 Strand,
London WC2R 0RL, England • Penguin Ireland, 25 St. Stephen's Green, Dublin 2,
Ireland (a division of Penguin Books Ltd) • Penguin Group (Australia), 250 Camberwell Road, Camberwell, Victoria 3124, Australia (a division of Pearson Australia
Group Pty Ltd) • Penguin Books India Pvt Ltd, 11 Community Centre, Panchsheel
Park, New Delhi - 110 017, India • Penguin Group (NZ), 67 Apollo Drive, Rosedale,
North Shore 0632, New Zealand (a division of Pearson New Zealand Ltd) • Penguin
Books (South Africa) (Pty) Ltd, 24 Sturdee Avenue, Rosebank, Johannesburg 2196,
South Africa • Penguin Books Ltd, Registered Offices: 80 Strand, London WC2R
0RL, England

The publisher does not have any control over and does not assume any responsibility
for author or third-party websites or their content.

Designed by Peonia Vázquez-D'Amico
Text set in Goudy Old Style
Printed in the U.S.A.

10 9 8 7 6 5 4 3 2 1

Library of Congress Cataloging-in-Publication Data
Dionne, Erin, date.
Models don't eat chocolate cookies / by Erin Dionne.
p. cm.
Summary: Overweight thirteen-year-old Celeste begins a campaign to lose weight in
order to make sure she does not win the Miss HuskyPeach modeling challenge, which
her mother and aunt have entered her in—against her wishes.
ISBN 978-0-8037-3296-4
[1. Overweight persons—Fiction. 2. Weight control—Fiction. 3. Models (Persons)—
Fiction. 4. Friendship—Fiction. 5. Self-esteem—Fiction. 6. Schools—Fiction.]
I. Title. II. Title: Models do not eat chocolate cookies.
PZ7.D6216Mo 2009
[Fic]—dc22
2008020612

For Frank, with all my love.

You were right.

• • •

Chapter 1

"NO WAY," I hissed through the slatted dressing room door. "I am not coming out."

"Honey, I have to see how it fits," Mom said. "Let me look."

I dropped my forehead against the beige cubicle wall. I'd have to give in eventually, but I wasn't opening up until my cousin was back in the clothing cubby next to me.

"Oh, angel! It's just bee-yoo-ti-ful on you. Isn't she a sight, Noelle?" Aunt Doreen's nasal whine came over the top of my dressing room door like arrows over a castle wall. Of course the dress was "bee-yoo-ti-ful" on Kirsten. What wasn't? She was tall, blond, athletic, and one of the nicest people I knew. She also shared my celebrity crush on singer Theo Christmas. We both fell in love with him when her older sister took us to see him in concert last summer. I swear, he was singing to me the whole time. (She disagrees.)

"Does it look okay from the back?" Kirsten asked. I imagined her pirouetting in front of the three-way mirror at the end of the row, hair twirling like a shampoo commercial, evenly tanned skin standing out against the back of the dress, pastel lace and fabric hugging her in all the right places. I chose the only dressing room without a mirror on purpose.

"It's lovely," my mother offered, her voice tight. "Will you come *out*?" she stage-whispered through the dressing room door. "This is ridiculous."

"Where's Celeste?" Aunt Doreen said. "I haven't seen her yet. Celeste, do you need help in there?"

I cringed. "No, Auntie, I'm fine," I called. "Just, uh, almost ready. One more minute." I tugged at the dress, hoping for the magical yank that would straighten seams, smooth wrinkles, or snap it into the right proportion. Sometimes you don't need a mirror to know when things are *very* wrong.

"Kirsten, turn around again. I think it needs hemming, don't you?" Aunt Doreen said. "Let's get that seamstress in here." Then, louder, directed at me, "Okay, Celeste, we're waiting."

Ready or not, here I come, I thought. Sliding the door's bolt back, I hiked up the skirt and stepped into the dressing room corridor, head high. Maybe it wasn't as bad as it felt.

Aunt Doreen gasped, then covered her mouth as if to trap what might follow. I let the dress sag to the floor.

"It's . . . Oh, honey," Mom tried. "It needs some alterations."

I could imagine.

"Some?" said Aunt Doreen, biting the word like a potato chip. "What size did you order?"

I hung my head, trying to dampen the zing of her words,

2

trying not to hear Mom explaining that we needed to order an adult size because the youth sizes weren't cut for me. Besides, Mom said, a seamstress could fix it so the dress would "fall right," whatever that meant.

"Wait!" barked a short white-haired woman with a tape measure around her neck and a handful of pins. She stood in the doorway between the dressing rooms and the rest of Angelique's Bridal Boutique. "Don't move or you'll tear the lace!" When she said it, though, "move" came out like "moof" and "the" sounded like "ze." I stayed put. Besides, where could I go in a falling-wrong dress?

"Zis needs several substantial alterations," she said, gesturing in my direction with her chin. "When is the wedding?"

"Nine weeks," Mom said, tearing her eyes away from me and turning to the seamstress. "Can it be fixed in time?"

Straight out of a soap opera, I thought. *I'm in critical condition.* I stared at my feet, lost in a puddle of apricot satin. Usually I avoided this type of situation—comfort was more important to me than fashion. Comfort meant clothes that didn't pull, ride up, or show off too much. Comfort was soft, cozy, and worn; not lacy, satiny, or peachy. A movement caught my eye. Kirsten, the Barbie Bridesmaid, was slipping into her dressing room. She raised her perfectly shaped eyebrows in an expression of sympathy before closing the door.

A bony hand pushed against the small of my back, and the seamstress ushered me to the carpet-covered platform in front of the three-way mirror Kirsten had just vacated. I hoisted myself up and thought, *I hate Kathleen.*

Kathleen was the bride. She's Kirsten's older sister, my oldest cousin. Ever since we moved to Los Alvios, California, five years ago, she'd watched me and my brother, Ben, when my parents went out or away for the weekend. I was flattered that she asked me to be a junior bridesmaid in her wedding, but once I saw the Peach Monstrosity, I wondered if my parents owed her babysitting money.

The dress was designed for someone like Kirsten. It had two layers sewn together down the length of the side seams. The bottom layer was fitted at the chest, with thin spaghetti straps holding the flimsy satin in place. The narrow waist dropped into a skinny skirt with a high slit in one leg and a mermaid-like swoosh of fabric in the back. The other layer was frothy peach lace that followed the shape of the satin, except the top had a scoop neck with elbow-length sleeves and slightly tufted shoulders.

Standing in front of the mirrors, I saw just how substantial those alterations would have to be.

I'm what you call "chubby" if you're nice, "fat" if you're like Lively Carson at school. Mom and Dad say that I haven't lost my baby fat. If that's the case at thirteen, I must have a lot of growing left to do. I'm short and round in the middle. And the bottom. Basically, I'm round all over, just like my dad. According to the way the dress fit, though, I'd once been six feet tall and had suddenly turned into a watermelon.

The lace constricted my upper chest and arms, forcing my pale skin through the pattern's openings. Blood pressure cuffs make looser sleeves, and I could see a purple line around each forearm under the seams. The fabric hung loosely over my chest, bunched at my belly and hips, and puddled around my feet. And the view was reflected over and over in the triple mirror in front of me.

This is why I always shop for myself, I thought, trying to avoid the multiple Celestes. I settled on staring at a spot above my own head. Mom complains that I buy the same stuff all the time when I'm at the mall with Sandra, my best friend. She says that my wardrobe "makes me look like a lump" and that I am "hiding my beauty under hoods and zippers." It's true that my closet is home to track pants and hoodies in a range of colors, but I know what looks good on me. When Mom gets fed up with my clothes, she brings home outfits for me to try on. Then she gets fed up with my labeling them "too tight," "too uncomfortable," or "showing too much" and returns them. This dress definitely fit multiple "too *something*" categories.

"We can take extra fabric from the bottom to make the side panels," the seamstress muttered as she buzzed around my feet, measuring here and pinning there. "The lace sleeves will be a challenge."

"It's my daughter's wedding," said Aunt Doreen, her voice climbing. "You have to make it fit."

"Mom," Kirsten called from her dressing room, "can you help me get out of this?" After a moment's hesitation, Aunt Doreen huffed to her aid.

The coil of anxiety that had been growing in my chest loosened. *Thanks, Kirsten,* I thought. Aunt Doreen was seconds from going nuclear.

I caught my mother's eyes in the mirror. Mom's got great

eyes—toffee-colored, with tiny green flecks that sparkle when she's angry or happy. I got my dad's eyes, kind of. His are dark brown, deep like chocolate, but mine resemble mud. Mom offered a smile that was supposed to be encouraging. I tried to smile back.

Kirsten, out of her dress and into a pink tank and jeans, hustled Aunt Doreen from the changing rooms and into the rest of the store.

When "ze" seamstress inserted the final pin and I was free from my reflection, I shuffled to my dressing room and wriggled out of the Monstrosity and into the day's blue hoodie and track pants. I wrapped my hair into a knot, hoisted my bag, and tried to forget the peach watermelon in the mirror.

Chapter 2

WHEN I LEFT the dressing room, I found Mom, Aunt Doreen, and Kirsten hovering around the dyeable shoes.

"It'll be fine, Doreen," Mom said, holding a pair of pumps. "The wedding's nine weeks away. Angelique does this all the time."

"I hope you're right," Aunt Doreen replied, "because that dress was not in good shape."

I coughed. *Do they think I'm deaf?* Okay, the dress looked awful on me, but how was that my fault? Why hadn't Kathleen thought of her roundest bridesmaid before she picked them out? I fumed, staring at the display.

"I hate it too, you know," whispered Kirsten, appearing at my side. "Who picks *lace?* Something from this decade would've been much better." She rolled her eyes at her sister's choice. Our moms moved their conversation closer to the cash register.

"But it looks good on *you,*" I protested. She didn't have to say stuff like that just to make me feel better, even though I was glad she did.

"So? Just because it looks good doesn't mean I have to like it. Actually—"

"Girls," Aunt Doreen called, "we're ready to leave. Let's go."

"Never mind," Kirsten said to me, waving at her mother. We made our way to the front of the store, dodging colorful racks of bridesmaid dresses and sparkly wedding gowns. Well, Kirsten dodged. I squeezed between the racks and knocked a dress off its hanger. My face warm, I struggled with the slippery material. Kirsten helped me replace it before the moms noticed. *Crisis avoided*, I thought. Aunt Doreen wouldn't have been able to leave without a full Fallen Dress Inspection.

We nearly bumped into them as we reached the door. Angelique's had a table just inside the entrance that was covered in flyers and brochures advertising community events, school concerts, and bridal shows. Mom and Aunt Doreen huddled together, peering at an orange flyer.

"It's perfect!" Aunt Doreen screeched, her voice reaching her nuclear register, only this time with happiness. "Five thousand dollars in scholarship money! And the chance to meet with an *agent*," she breathed, as though "an agent" was her favorite celebrity.

"What an opportunity," Mom agreed. Neither turned to see us behind them. Kirsten and I shot looks at each other.

"Mom?" Kirsten asked. "What're you looking at?"

Aunt Doreen spun like a top. "I'm looking at your future," she said, giving Kirsten a big smile. Aunt Doreen is what Mom likes to call "a nervous wreck." She gets stressed out over nothing and spends too much time worrying about other people's business. But when she gets excited about something, she doesn't let it go. Same when she gets upset. When Kathleen got engaged, Aunt Doreen cried for three days straight about "losing her angel to that *boy*," even though Kathleen and Paul had been together for years. Now, cheeks flushed, she thrust the orange page at us.

Across the top, in bold letters, it read: *Be a Model!! This is your chance to shine!* And, underneath: *Local catalog company looking for young women ages 12–16 to model our new line of active wear, formalwear, and sleepwear. Send recent full-body photo and headshot with contact information and parent or guardian signature to PeachWear Industries, 4567 South Market St., Suite 450, San Francisco. All submissions will be considered for the regional Miss HuskyPeach contest, winner eligible for $5,000 scholarship and a meeting with a representative from Torre Modeling Agency.*

Sounded perfect for Kirsten.

Evidently, she didn't think so, because she giggled.

"What is so funny, missy?" Aunt Doreen snapped, her voice dropping into the I'm-not-pleased range. "This is your *future*."

Based on that tone, I'm glad it's not mine. I stepped to the side to get some space from the developing circus—and to hide behind a rack if anyone I knew came in to shop.

"Really?" Kirsten chuckled. "*My* future? Are you sure?" Her giggles changed to laughter.

"What harm is there in sending your picture?" Mom asked. "I don't understand."

Kirsten rolled her eyes. "I don't think I have a chance,"

she explained. "It's really not for me. Besides, Kathleen did pageants, remember? I decided to swim."

What was she talking about?

"Kirsten Beth Lowry," Aunt Doreen said, her eyes turning to flint. "You are a beautiful girl. Why don't you want to take this opportunity?" She shook the flyer for emphasis.

Kirsten sighed. "Mom, it's not for me," she said again, looking uncomfortable. She twirled a piece of hair around one finger. "Do you know what PeachWear is?"

"It is a company offering you the chance to be a model," Aunt Doreen said, "I know *that.*"

Kirsten shook her head, sending her shampoo-commercial hair flying. She really could be a model if she wanted to. "They make clothes for, um, larger sized girls," she explained. Her eyes flicked over to me and she bit her lip. "You know that store in the mall, the HuskyPeach? That's this company."

My stomach went cold. *The HuskyPeach? That's where Mom goes on her Fed Up shopping sprees for me.*

Kirsten tilted her chin at the flyer. "I don't think they want me as their model."

That light in Aunt Doreen's eyes faded. Her face was as sad as a little kid watching a brand-new helium balloon float into the sky. "Oh," was all she said.

I let out a breath I didn't even know I was holding.

"The HuskyPeach?" Mom asked. "Really?" Her eyes slid past Aunt Doreen and focused on me.

The breath caught in my chest. Quickly, I shook my head. *No way,* I mouthed.

Mom's toffee eyes were joined by Aunt Doreen's blue ones.

Not the Double Sister Stare! This would not end well.

"Celeste," Aunt Doreen said, catching on, "we could send your photo in instead. Since Kathleen gave it up, we could have a model in the family again!" Her eyes gradually regained their light.

"This could be so good for you," Mom said. "Think of how fun it would be to be out there, wearing new clothes, being in a catalog. It's such an *opportunity*."

Now, I have to admit, being a model sounds like a pretty cool job. Flying to all parts of the world to have my picture taken, hanging out with stars, never going to school, making lots and lots of money . . . that would be great. I imagined myself on a beach with Theo Christmas, posing for a *Celeb Eye* magazine cover shoot. "Closer," the photographer would direct. "Theo, pull her *closer*." I'd rest my head against his chest and smile hugely for the camera.

And then my imagination showed me nestling with him in my polka-dot one-piece, the one with the "modesty skirt" Grandma got me, to hide what she calls my "peasant" shape. Modeling might be fun, or a great opportunity, but being the face of a clothing line for chunky girls was not the type of modeling that would generate seaside celebrity photo sessions. Excessive junior high teasing? Probably. Snuggles with Theo Christmas? No way. Also, husky or not, models don't eat chocolate cookies. I sighed.

Mom and Aunt Doreen were watching me like all of a sudden I was going to grow six inches and turn into Kirsten.

"Um, I don't think that'd be a good idea, Auntie," I said,

the burn of shame from her earlier words about the state of my dress rekindled. "I'm not cut out to be the model in the family."

Aunt Doreen's eyes narrowed. "Think of the scholarship money, Celeste."

"And you could put it on your applications as an activity," Mom said, rereading the flyer. "You don't have any."

I wanted to point out that since I hadn't even started high school, college scholarships or applications weren't really on my radar screen, but my stomach was churning and my cheeks felt hot. How could I ever get on a stage and show off my "full figure"? I turned to Mom, raising my eyebrows and hoping she'd get the hint that it was time to leave. Unfortunately, she was focused on that orange piece of paper. The top of her head was not much help.

"Mom," Kirsten interrupted, shifting from foot to foot, "can we go? I'm going to be late for practice."

Aunt Doreen glanced at her watch. "Swim practice begins at eight," she said. "It's not even five yet."

"I know, but I have a Spanish test tomorrow and need to review my vocab tonight." Kirsten leaned against the door, opening it an inch at a time. "I don't know all my verbs."

Mom gave me a last pleading glance. I scowled.

With a reluctant shake of her head, Mom placed the flyer back on the table. Kirsten held the door open and we filed into the parking lot, Aunt Doreen bringing up the rear. I thought I saw a flash of orange as she dug through her purse for the car keys, but once we were in the car, I was just glad to be leaving both the Monstrosity and all that peachness behind.

Chapter 3

I'D TOLD SANDRA about the Peach Monstrosity during our nightly phone call, and a week later it was still our main topic of conversation. She and I had been best friends since Chuckie Swift poured glue in our hair in third-grade art class. We first bonded over the school nurse's scrubbing, and our friendship was sealed during detention in the principal's office after she punched Chuckie and I cheered her on. She agreed that Kathleen could have picked a better bridesmaid dress.

"You've been talking about it like it's the worst thing ever. But, you know," she said, making loud smacking noises into the phone, "it doesn't sound too bad." Addicted to sour apple Jolly Rancher candies, Sandra sounded as though she was walking through mud puddles when she paused or stopped talking. Gross, but I'd gotten used to it. I organized six Oreos into a stack on the edge of my nightstand.

"What's not too bad?" I winced at a loud slurp. The candy clicked against her teeth.

"The dress. It sounds like the style is cute." I could tell she was stifling a giggle.

"Yeah, if you're six thousand feet tall and into dressing like a frothy dessert." The stack became stairs. Two fingers climbed the cookies. Seeing who could top the other was one of our favorite conversation games. We'd been doing it forever.

"Or if it were the turn of the century." Smack, slurp, slurp.

"Or if I were a mermaid queen who wanted to live in the desert."

A pause. "What *is* too bad—with your coloring, the peach should look really cute on you."

"Yeah, but it doesn't."

"Obviously." She clicked the candy against her teeth in an extra-long silence. "You're not the right shape for it either."

"No one is the right shape for this dress. Kirsten barely looks good in it." My fingers tap-danced on my Oreo stack. A wiggling sensation, similar to the one I felt when listening to Aunt Doreen at Angelique's, crept through my belly. Where was Sandra going with this?

"If you weren't as round . . ." Her voice trailed off.

A zap, like a bee sting, pricked my heart. My cookie climbing ceased. *"Weren't as round?"* I repeated, coughing the words out.

A pause in the slurping, then the smacks came faster. "Uh, well, you know. Your shape just makes it harder to fit."

"Mmm," I answered, not trusting my voice to sound normal. I guess Sandra took it as an invitation to keep going.

"I mean, if you paid more attention to your look . . ."

"*What?*" I squawked. So much for normal. A bomb of hurt burst in my chest.

From Sandra's end there was a loud crack. She'd split the candy, something I knew she did only when she was nervous. I didn't care. I was too busy trying to pick up the shards of my exploded feelings.

Where did that come from? Sandra shared my love for caramel sundaes and cookies; they just didn't stick to her the same way they stuck to me. She never said anything about my size . . . *or hadn't until recently.* Sandra had always spoken up for me; she said and did things to take care of us both. I just watched from the sidelines and stayed out of the way. All through elementary school, she'd threaten to beat people up if they were mean to me. Once junior high rolled around, though, things changed. She seemed to get annoyed with me, especially lately. And she was saying less and less when Lively made fun of me—no matter how out of the way I stayed.

"It's just . . . I don't know. Maybe people wouldn't say stuff to you if you tried something new with your look once in a while." Her helpful tone grated on my wounds.

"*People,*" I said, filling my words with sarcasm in an effort to hide the hurt burning my chest, "shouldn't be saying anything about my look. Especially people like Lively Carson. I'd rather be comfortable than mean any day."

"She's not mean to everyone."

"You're *defending* Lively Carson? Are you serious?" If Sandra told me she was moving to China, I wouldn't have been as shocked.

"You're right. Forget it. I'm sorry." Her words came quick and tight. The Jolly Rancher wrapper crinkled in the background.

"Sure," I muttered, not wanting a fight. Pushing the issue wouldn't make anything better. As a distraction, I pried the top off an Oreo and licked at its sugary filling.

"Anyway, did you see Robbie Flan today?"

"Mm-hmm." I wasn't ready for words. *Why was Sandra so interested in my appearance all of a sudden? And why was she defending* Lively?

"He was wearing a baseball hat at lunch." Sandra's crush on Robbie started when they were paired to work on a social studies map project in the fall. Each night, we spent lots of phone time trying to figure out how she could get his attention. Unfortunately for her, our plan of sliding one-letter notes into his locker that spelled "I LIKE YOU" backfired when Sandra wouldn't sign her name to the last one. Robbie thought Joanie Purcell was his admirer. I let her speculate about where Robbie got his hat and why he'd risk getting a dress code demerit for wearing it, while I sorted my emotional debris.

During the day, I stayed away from Robbie and his friends—from many of the boys at school, actually. They called me "Burrito Grande." Theo Christmas, smiling down from his poster on my wall, never compared me to an oozy overstuffed food item. Or said anything about my "look." I smiled at him, and he grinned back, all dark curls and smoky eyes. *Bet* he'd *like me no matter what I looked like. Or wore.* Then Sandra's older brother, Geoff, yelled at her to get off the phone.

"He wants to talk to his *girl*friend," Sandra said, stretching the word out like taffy. "Ow!" The scuffling sounds floated over the receiver. "I'm hanging *up*!" she shouted. Things settled down, and she resumed her Jolly Rancher clacking.

"Don't forget about PE tomorrow," she said. "It's important."

"Why?" The word came out sharper than I'd intended. Sandra felt it her duty to never let me forget my PE clothes. Tonight I didn't appreciate the reminder.

Sandra didn't seem to notice. "Part one of the physical fitness test." Suck, smack, slurp.

I groaned. One more thing to wreck this week. We'd suffered through the Fitness Challenge twice a year, once in the fall, once in the spring, since fifth grade. The gym teachers at Albert J. Hancock Memorial Middle School—AlHo to its students—kept records on our year-to-year progress through sit-ups, push-ups, hanging on a bar, and, my least favorite, Running the Mile. Every time I hit the track, I fell into the "needs improvement/no progress made" category. Sandra always scored in the top ten percent.

"Can't wait," I said. Sandra squealed again, and our conversation was over.

After hanging up, I realized that I still hadn't told her about the modeling flyer. I never could seem to get around to it. Better not to bring up Miss HuskyPeach tonight anyway, I decided, especially after her comments. Instead, cookie by cookie, I dismantled the rest of my tower and munched under Theo Christmas's sympathetic eyes.

Want one? I split a cookie and offered the top to my poster.

Have them all, he replied with a smile. *Each and every one.*

An hour later, I was curled up on my bed with *The Lord of the Flies* (for Language Arts) and a bag of Butter Brothers Extra Butter microwave popcorn (because you need snacks if you're stuck on a deserted island and your best friend is acting like a jerk) when I heard a giant *slam!* and the house shook.

"Noelle!" My dad's voice boomed through the house like summer thunder. Not good. When Dad yells, something is very wrong. "Noelle! Let's go!"

Scurrying footsteps came from my parents' room.

"Wes?" For a moment, Mom sounded squeaky, like Aunt Doreen. I propped my book next to the popcorn and slid off my bed. A peek into the hall showed Mom bolting down the stairs wearing the green and pink striped bathrobe she changed into after dinner.

Dad lowered his voice and I couldn't hear. Then, louder, "Celeste!"

I leaned over the banister. "Yeah?"

"Ben's at Goodwin Memorial, sweetheart. Mom and I are going over there now."

"What happened this time?"

Dad shook his head. Behind him, Mom traded her bathrobe for one of his fleece jackets from the front hall closet. She was still in her paisley pajamas and slippers. "I wish you'd remembered to bring your cell phone with you," she muttered.

"Fly ball. Caught it with his noggin instead of his glove. He's getting X-rays," Dad said to me, jingling his keys. "Coach Anchor is with him."

"That's a first," I said, as Mom disappeared from sight, then returned with her purse.

"That's what I'm worried about," she said, fishing through the bag. She held up her cell phone for me to see. "I'm ready."

"We'll be back in a couple of hours," Dad said over his shoulder. From where I stood, his bald spot and protruding belly made him look like the number eight. "Don't open the door to anyone, okay?"

I nodded, knowing he couldn't see me. Not like this scene was anything unusual anyway.

Ben's spent more time in casts, slings, braces, wraps, and Band-Aids than any kid I know. He's broken his nose twice, and his wrist, one big toe, and a finger once each. The last time we added them up, he'd received 159 stitches. When we first moved, the school called social services on my parents, thinking they were abusive. Then they saw Ben on the playground.

"Make sure you pack your schoolbag for tomorrow," Mom called. From above, with Mom's thin frame and Dad's round one, they made an eighteen. I nodded again, but the door had closed.

Back in my room, I plopped on my bed and propped the popcorn on my stomach. I tried to dredge up more than average concern for Ben. *What if this accident really rocked his brain? What if he goes blind or something? Could you go blind from being hit with a baseball?* I turned to Theo for an answer, but he just sat, arm slung around his guitar, contemplating the microphone.

You're not helping me feel any better.

I sighed. Even with all that could happen, when your parents spend more time in the ER with your brother than watching the show on TV, it's hard to be dramatic.

I paged through *The Lord of the Flies*, but put it down when I felt like Piggy was getting what he deserved. Plus, I was out of popcorn and parched. A trip to the kitchen was in order.

Downstairs, a frosty mug of root beer in hand, I wandered around the family room trying not to be bored. On my second lap, I stopped in front of Mom's desk. Its surface was covered by piles of paper and receipts; she spent about a half hour there every night after dinner, paying bills and sorting our lives. I poked at the stacks, idly glancing at a grocery receipt ($93.34) and the permission slip for Ben's class field trip to the planetarium.

Bet he saw stars tonight, I thought. Then I felt bad.

A glossy corner with a ragged edge stuck out from under the permission slip. I tugged and a page torn from a magazine slid from the pile. "Creative Cruciferous Creations: Snazzy Cauliflower, Broccoli, and Brussels Sprouts Recipes Your Family Will LOVE!" The photo showed a casserole dish of dark-green lumps lurking in a bubbling batter.

Oh, no. Mom cannot have this in the house, I thought. For the past few weeks, she had been trying to liven up our vegetable intake and get us to eat healthier. Okay, get *me* to eat healthier. Dad and Ben never saw a food item they didn't like—green, leafy, or otherwise. Rabbit food doesn't do it for me. Why nibble broccoli when you can eat potatoes? They're both vegetables. Salad is okay, and corn, but I can pretty much guarantee that a "Creative Cruciferous Creation" is going to taste as good as stew made from soggy weeds and dirt. Tossing the recipe would benefit the whole family. I stood over the garbage can and ceremoniously dropped it. The recipe fluttered from side to side as it fell and, true to my athletic powers, missed.

I bent and scooped it off the floor. As I was about to stuff it in the can, the headline "Be Model Thin in Four Weeks!" on the back of the recipe made me pause. The ad featured a woman whose waist looked as big around as my pinkie, and her red bathing suit was cut up high and down low. I didn't need much imagination to see the wonders this diet worked on her.

It was simple: The ingredient list included prune juice, carrot juice, lemons, egg whites, and a few others. You mixed it together, drank it twice a day, and, according to the woman, "the weight just fell off." I glanced down at my snug XL pajama bottoms, rolled so I wouldn't trip over the long legs. *Really?* Still standing over the trash can, I told myself, *This is stupid. That stuff never works. It'll taste awful.* But I didn't move or throw the page away. I took a swig of root beer and closed my eyes as I swallowed.

As the sweet soda slid down my throat, I saw myself wearing the Monstrosity, reflected again and again in Angelique's dressing room mirror, and heard Aunt Doreen's

"What size did you order?" followed by Sandra's comment about my shape, and her not-so-helpful suggestion to change my look so "people" wouldn't say stuff about me.

It's not like dieting had never occurred to me, but it seemed as though I never *absolutely* needed to go on one. In elementary school, where everyone had a little baby fat, weight didn't matter—someone always hung out with me on the playground. But instead of disappearing when I reached junior high, my "baby fat" grew with me and all of a sudden things were different: There weren't as many people to sit with at lunch when Sandra wasn't around. Lively Carson made me her favorite target. When I was a seventh grader, a group of boys yelled "Wide load approaching!" when I came down the hall. That did not help my social status. And after today's Self-Esteem Explosion, a diet drink seemed like the perfect solution. When I opened my eyes, the woman in the red bathing suit was smiling at me. *You can do it*, her eyes urged. *Try it! Be like me!*

I imagined being able to eat like Sandra and look like the bathing suit model instead of a beach ball, like Dad. Next, I imagined what it would be like to *like* my reflection in the triple mirror, or buy something other than track pants and not have to worry about my "look." Instead of "Burrito Grande," I'd be the Eensy Enchilada, the Teensy Tortilla. At the very least, people wouldn't tease me.

Why not? Depositing the ad on the counter, I scavenged the kitchen in search of the blender. Behind the pots and pans? Nope. In the cabinet with the old coffeemaker? Not there either. With the help of a chair from the kitchen table,

I found it in the cabinet over the fridge. Then I dug out most of the ingredients, lining them up on the island.

After a couple of false starts getting the blender bucket to fit the base properly, I went to work mixing, measuring, and pureeing. We didn't have everything the recipe listed, so I swapped limes for the lemons and fudged a few others: mayo for egg whites (close enough) and balsamic vinegar for apple cider vinegar. Besides, is there really a huge difference between tomato paste and tomato juice? Doubt it. My completed concoction was dark brown, gloppy, and appeared about as appetizing as the picture of the Brussels sprouts recipe. Actually, it looked a lot like root beer—if root beer was chunky instead of fizzy.

I needed a spoon to nudge the ploppy chunkiness from the pitcher into a glass. When I held it up to the light, I couldn't see through it. *Definitely* not *root beer. They should show you a picture of what it's supposed to look like when it's done,* I thought, alarmed by its murky color. The ad woman smiled at me. *Go for it!* she encouraged.

I took a deep breath, held my nose, drank, and swallowed. And swallowed some more, trying to empty the glass. It tasted *nothing* like the sugary zing of root beer. I retched, bracing myself over the sink. My stomach rolled, then clenched tight, and for a minute I thought I was going to yurk. I counted backward from ten, taking slow, shallow breaths like Dad taught me when I had the flu, and gradually my stomach settled.

I guess the weight "just falls off" because it tastes so nasty you don't ever want to eat or drink anything again. I rinsed my mouth, but the aftertaste—spoiled coleslaw—coated the back of my throat. I'd need a toothbrush with a handle as long as a rake to get back there and scrub my tonsils if I ever wanted to enjoy dinner again.

"You suck," I muttered at the red bathing suit model. Then I squished her and tossed her in the garbage can for good. It didn't make the taste go away.

After cleaning up the experiment, I held my nose and poured what was left of the concoction into a travel mug. An odd-smelling garbage can might inspire questions I didn't want to answer.

I'll dump it out at school, I thought. Once finished, I packed my backpack and got ready for bed.

Then the cramps started. They came in waves: three or four hot squeezes of pain, and then my belly would be fine again. Until the next round. I lay in bed, waiting for them to pass, listening for my parents to return with Ben, hating Skimpy Red Bathing Suit Woman and the Peach Monstrosity. Regardless of my look, or what was said about it, being a wide-load grande *anything* certainly *felt* a lot better than being a diet-drinking, tiny-bathing-suit-wearing almost-yurker.

Change was not worth this.

Chapter 4

AT BREAKFAST THE next morning (which I barely ate—clearly, the Diet Drink of Horror was still doing its job), Mom told me that Ben had a mild concussion and would need to stay home from school.

"He'll have an awful headache for a few days, but he'll be fine," she said, stirring a pan of scrambled eggs. "Want some?" she continued, tilting the pan in my direction.

Nauseated by the smell, I shook my head and hurried to get out the door.

"They're gooood," Ben taunted. His smile revealed egg in his teeth. Some slipped out and splattered his T-shirt.

"Gross!" My stomach rolled at the disgusting sight, but even though eating didn't appeal to me, I was jealous that he was staying home.

My stomach finally settled halfway through my first class. When the passing period bell rang, I slid from my seat, grateful to be feeling better. I was so grateful that I forgot to close my backpack, and spilled the contents of the big pocket. *Lord of the Flies,* my social studies book, and my notebook skidded across the floor. My face hot, I bent into the crush of kids and fumbled for my stuff.

"Whoa, Supremo Grande, you're blocking the exit," one of the boys cackled.

"That's a fire hazard," another joked. I pushed my books into my bag as fast as I could and kept my eyes to the floor as I bumped my way into the hall.

By second-period break, the "Supremo" reference had revived the Gaggle of Negative Comments from the night before. I stood in front of my locker, listening to the crowd of whispers in my head, searching for my Emergency Twinkie Stash, when my hand closed around the smooth plastic of the travel mug. I hadn't dumped the drink yet.

Maybe it's better the next day, I reasoned, *like spaghetti sauce.* As nice as it sounded, I doubted my own logic. There was no way that glop would taste any better, plus it made my stomach do the mambo when it was fresh. And wasn't there some mom-warning about mayonnaise spoiling fast? I debated.

"Hey! Look! It's a solar eclipse!" Lively Carson's excited voice sounded behind me. Without thinking, I spun around.

"Oh, it's just Celeste. Never mind." She flicked her hand like she was brushing a fly away and kept walking. The girls following her were laughing hard enough to pee themselves.

Debate over. I brought the mug to my lips. The cover kept

the aroma from escaping, at least. Before I could lose my nerve, I slugged down the rest of the concoction in big gulps.

I bolted for a water fountain. It hadn't aged well.

"You're not looking too good today," Sandra said as we met in the hall a few minutes later and walked to gym, our first shared class.

"Not feeling too good," I responded, stifling a burp.

"Do you need to—"

"Oh no," I said, cutting her off, and froze. Sandra walked into my backpack. We had just crossed the threshold of the girls' locker room.

"Are you okay?" she asked, concerned. She raised her voice over the slamming lockers. "What's up? Did you forget your clothes? I reminded you last night!"

"I wish," I said. "It's the Fitness Challenge that I forgot about. Tell me we don't have to run today."

Sandra plopped her backpack on the narrow wooden bench between the rows of lockers. "Can't tell you that. We're running the mile."

My stomach flipped a cartwheel. I groaned.

"Maybe Coach will let you out of it," she said. "Get changed and talk to her. I'll go with you, if you want." She tossed her shirt into her locker.

Not a chance, I wanted to say. I much preferred reading to running, lounging to laps, and Coach Anapoli knew it. I bent to my lock, twisting the combination while figuring out what I was going to say.

Sandra stood in her bra and jeans, unfolding her gym

shirt before putting it on. Sandra never experienced embarrassment. While other girls (including me) would tug our arms out of shirts, hunch over, pull our gym shirts over our heads and pull the other shirts out through the neck, Sandra just took everything off like she was in her bedroom at home. If I looked like her, I wouldn't care either. Small and athletic, Sandra didn't have any fat on her body. She also had just the right amount of something to fill her bra with—not a lot of something, but enough. On the other hand, I was always trying to hide too much of something.

I squirmed into my gym clothes, then shoved my schoolbag into my locker and slammed it. Coach Anapoli made the girls sit in the unused shower area while she took attendance and made announcements. The green tile floor was cold and dirty-looking, even though no one had showered in the room for years. I squeezed into a corner, leaning against the sticky wall tiles, still tasting the Diet Drink of Horror. Sandra went to get me a cup of water. Across the room, Millicent Taposok and Katy O'Sullivan, who Sandra and I ate lunch with, waved. I managed a weak smile in their direction. My stomach shuddered.

In front of me, Lively Carson and her friends huddled together, giggling, probably about the "solar eclipse" in the hall. Lively was AlHo's Miss Matchy Perfect—her barrettes matched her earrings, which matched her shorts, which matched her socks. I'm sure, if I cared to stick my head down her locker row when she was changing, I'd see that her underwear matched everything too. For all her matchiness, though, Lively's personality didn't coordinate with her designed appearance. Her favorite sport? Being mean to everyone except her special group of friends—who she complimented constantly, if they met her standards.

The group giggle-fest over, I watched as she mocked Carlee Morgenstern—one of her supposed friends—about the new way she was wearing her hair, in a French braid. After a few minutes of incessant teasing, Carlee switched it back to the Lively-approved ponytail. Revolting.

Sandra came back with my water, but before we could talk to Coach Anapoli together she sent Sandra to set up cones. The other girls whispered on our walk down to the track, eyes sliding toward me every so often. My stomach churned.

Coach divided us into five groups of twelve (gym was not only a double class period, it was twice the size of a regular class). While one group ran laps, the other four would play soccer or field hockey against one another. Sandra wasn't on my team. Instead, Millie, Katy, and I—three of the worst athletes in our class—made basic attempts to provide field hockey defense. Not that anyone was playing an actual game—they were just knocking the ball around enough so Coach wouldn't make us do extra laps.

"Oh look," Lively said as she jogged by on her way to the track, her group summoned by Coach Anapoli's whistle, "it's the Barnyard Squad: Cow, Pig, and Horse!" She mooed and snorted as she passed.

"Cretin," Katy whispered under her breath. Tall, with a long face, Katy was a science brain. She was enrolled in an accelerated program, so she took high school science classes in the afternoon. Lucky.

Millicent nodded, pink scrunchie bouncing in her dark hair. "Can't stand her." She'd earned her nickname for wearing something pink every day. I guess having a favorite color was not high on Lively's List of Cool.

I was about to join in when another cramp, this one epic in comparison to the ones I'd had the night before, hit my stomach like a boa constrictor squeezing a jungle explorer. I doubled over my stick.

"Celeste? You okay?" Katy asked. Her eyebrows made a deep V over her nose.

I shook my head. "Stomach," I gasped. Sweat popped up on my forehead. I tried to breathe, regretting every drop of that drink.

"We should tell Coach," Millicent said.

As soon as she got the words out, the tweet of Anapoli's whistle pierced the air around the track. "Group three!" she shouted. "You're up!"

"That's us," said Katy. "Do you need help?" Around us, the rest of our group dropped their sticks and headed toward the starting line.

Some short, shallow breaths helped. "I'm okay," I said, and repeated myself to be sure. "I'm okay." The cramp loosened its hold.

"Ladies, let's move it!" Coach Anapoli shouted. "What are you doing, grazing?" I swore I heard Lively laughing. I trudged to the starting line, then over to Coach herself. Sandra waved encouragement from the sidelines.

Supposedly one of a pair of identical twins, Coach Anapoli stood about six feet tall. Rumor had it that she was such a good basketball player in college that she cut her hair short and tried out for the NBA. Rumor also had it that she only washed her blue tracksuit every two weeks. No one wanted to get close enough to find out the truth. What I *did* know was that she hated me. I was a big soup of things she despised: quiet, clumsy, uncoordinated, and chubby.

"Coach, I, uh, really don't feel good," I began.

"Don't want to hear it, Harris." She didn't even look up from her clipboard.

"But it's my stomach," I tried. "It really—"

"Don't care. I'm sure you'll be fine after you run." She held up her stopwatch. "Get in line."

My twisting guts felt heavy. I sighed and lined up. *Four laps. Walk if you want.*

When I glanced at Coach Anapoli, she held the stopwatch at the ready. "On your mark, get set . . . GO!" she barked.

I went. Millie and Katy tucked their elbows close to their sides and were soon far ahead of me. The weight in my guts leaked into my legs, and a heavy, shivery sensation crept through my body. Sweat rolled down my back and forehead, dripping into my eyes. *Halfway done with lap one—halfway done with lap one*, I chanted. As I rounded the home stretch of the first lap, Joanie Purcell passed me, finishing her third.

I dropped my head, pumped my arms, and willed my legs to move faster. A cramp clawed my side.

"Mooo! Mooo!" Lively Carson waved her field hockey stick to get my attention—as if her barnyard noises wouldn't. "Moooove it, Celeste!"

I clenched my fists and pushed harder. *Halfway through with lap two—halfway through with lap two,* I repeated. Never mind that everyone else in my group, including Katy and Millie, had passed me, and Joanie Purcell was *done.* I just wanted to finish and get it over with. All the while, my pounding heart, rolling stomach, and heaving lungs competed to see which would explode first.

At my fastest, I moved no quicker than a slow jog. I reached Coach Anapoli at the starting line and began my third lap. "Fifteen-oh-four," she shouted, as another runner bounded past and finished. I forced my legs to keep moving and clutched my side.

Almost free of lap three—the words' rhythm echoed my footsteps. Head thumping, lungs burning, I rounded the turn closest to the starting line. The rest of my group—done—were clustered around the edge of the track, leaning against one another as they caught their breath. Group four also watched, waiting for me to clear the track so they could start their run. I swiped stinging sweat from my eyes. *Hope they don't think I'm crying,* I thought. Although I probably would have been in tears if I wasn't concentrating so hard on not dying.

"Let's go, Harris!" Coach hollered as I approached. She moved to the edge of the track to yell my time as I passed.

This is supposed to be encouraging? Anyone who wasn't watching turned in my direction. *Great.* The boys' class was returning to the gym, carrying football equipment. A few of them stopped to catch the show. Even through my blurry vision, their pointing fingers were hard to miss. I didn't think it was possible to feel any worse, but I did.

My heart thudded like a tennis ball down a flight of stairs.

As I got closer to Coach Anapoli, time turned funny. Everything slowed. I felt each foot land on the track. My ears rushed and roared with the sound of blood pumping through my head. Katy and Millie stood to one side, heads down and taking deep breaths, recovering. Hockey sticks swung and soccer balls bounced as my classmates watched. Coach raised her stopwatch as I crossed the line to start lap four.

"Twen—" she began. Behind her, Lively Carson and some of the boys—Robbie Flan among them—snickered. Farther down the track, Sandra raised her hand to me in another wave. Blood thumped behind my eyes.

My stomach heaved.

"Oh—" Coach Anapoli continued. My stomach heaved again, and I staggered to the side of the track—toward Coach Anapoli. Spit filled my mouth. I burped—a loud one—and my belly flipped. I hiccupped and clasped a hand over my lips. Coach's eyes widened.

"Oooh," I gasped. I clutched my belly with both hands.

"Harris!" she snapped. "Get—" But I didn't hear the rest. A geyser erupted in my middle, and there's no stopping Mother Nature.

I yurked.

On Coach Anapoli's shoes.

"Oh *crap!*" she shouted.

If it were fizzy and not so chunky, it could have been root beer.

Chapter 5

AFTER SANDRA ESCORTED me to the nurse's office, chiding me for eating a "heavy snack" before gym (there was *no way* I was admitting what I'd downed before class), I spent the next two class periods on the couch, resting, and begging Nurse Callahan not to call my mom. Explaining what happened would only bring humiliation and questions I didn't want to answer. And that outweighed spending the rest of the day in bed, listening to Theo Christmas and napping.

On my way home that afternoon I felt about as low as a spider's knees, and just as ugly. As I turned onto our street, I saw Mom sitting on the front steps of our house. She was never outside when I got home. My heart picked up speed. *She knows. Nurse Callahan did call her.* I walked faster. She stood and waved as I approached.

"Honey, it's great!" she called across the lawn.

She doesn't know. I slowed down, puffing for air.

She met me halfway. "I didn't open it, honey, but I'm so excited. Imagine, you going behind our back like this. It's got to be good news, right? They got back to you so quickly, and it's a thick envelope."

"What do you mean?" I stopped and plopped my schoolbag on the lawn.

She smiled a big Mom smile. "Don't tease, Celeste. I'm proud that you sent it on your own. It's okay." She waggled a pastel-colored envelope and held it out to me.

"I didn't *send* anything," I protested, not taking the package.

She let out an exasperated huff of air and shook the envelope. "Just open it."

I reached out. *Ms. Celeste Harris*, I read above our address. When I flipped it over, I saw *PeachWear Industries, 4567 South Market St., Suite 450, San Francisco, CA 94105.*

"Mom, I really don't know what this is about." I gestured with the envelope.

She sighed, and the Impatient Crease folded between her eyebrows. "Fine, Celeste. If you want to open it privately, that's fine. Just let me know what it says." She turned, back stiff, and marched into the house.

What the heck is this? My brain wouldn't make the full picture—I recognized the return address on the envelope, but couldn't figure out how they found me.

Maybe it's a coupon, I thought. But if it was a coupon, why was I still standing on my front lawn, staring at the envelope and afraid to open it? I took a deep breath and slid my index finger under the flap. "Oh!" I blurted. Paper cut. I kissed my finger, licking away the blood. The envelope fluttered to my feet when I removed the contents: pastel-colored stationery and a puff of perfume.

Congratulations, Ms. C. Harris! said the typed page.

You've been selected to represent PeachWear Industries as a contestant in the Northern California Regional PeachWear Modeling Challenge. You will have the opportunity to participate in a catalog photo shoot, walk the runway, meet with our hair and makeup experts, and finally show us that you could be the face of the HuskyPeach in a San Francisco Fashion Show!

My lungs got confused and stopped working. I couldn't breathe. I tilted my head to the sky and sucked in a big gulp of air. *It couldn't have said "you've been selected."* I reread the letter to make sure I read it wrong in the first place.

I hadn't. There were forms to fill out, a calendar of events, and a brochure with the latest catalog design and a big YOUR FACE HERE where the model would be.

But instead of picturing MY FACE THERE, all I saw were Lively and her posse from school, ponytails bobbing, fingers pointing. And what I heard was more moos.

Mom poked her head out of the kitchen as soon as she heard me close the front door, her eyebrows raised in a question mark. I dropped my backpack on the floor.

"I'm a contestant," I said. My voice sounded as flat as a pancake.

Mom let out a whoop, the kind when Ben hits a home run instead of his head. She swooped me into a squeeze.

"That's wonderful," she said. "Everyone will see how special you are."

Exactly.

When she finally let me go, she ushered me to the kitchen table, where we both sat and she read the letter herself. Her eyes welled up with tears. "I'm so proud of you, Celeste."

My heart dropped. I didn't want to disappoint her, but I couldn't stand the humiliation of being a HuskyPeach. *How did this day get* worse?

"Mom, really, I didn't do this. Honest. I didn't *want* to be part of this. I still don't." Being a fat model would just be a new and different way to be tormented at school. But Mom didn't seem to care. The way she was acting, it was like I was a *real* modeling contestant.

Mom's eyes turned cloudy and she gave her head a tight shake. "Celeste, what do you mean? *Look* at this." She gestured at the itinerary and plans. "A fashion show, a photo shoot, and a chance to walk the runway. This is so exciting!"

"I don't want to do that stuff, Mom." I swallowed hard. "I don't want to be a fat model. This wasn't my plan." My eyes filled with tears for what felt like the millionth time that day.

"Honey, then why'd you enter?" she said, covering my hand with her own. "You're a beautiful girl, no matter what your size. You know that's what your father and I think. You should be proud of this. Not everyone gets this type of opportunity. You will shine."

Yeah, well not everyone wants *to be a chubby teen model*, I thought. I wiped my eyes and sniffled. "I didn't enter. And I don't feel pretty."

"You need to think about this. You'll see, once you get used to the idea you'll be so excited." Mom moved from the table. She wasn't hearing me at all. "Dad will be thrilled for you. We'll wait and tell him when he gets home."

"Mom, I don't know," I said, imagining the horror of parading across a stage in front of strangers in a Chunky Chick Contest. The picture was terrible. "Mom, I don't think—" I began, but the ringing phone cut me off. Ignoring my earlier Explosive Yurking, I escaped to the pantry to grab some cookies and force the unpleasant images from my head while Mom reached for the receiver.

"Doreen! You'll never guess what exciting news Celeste received today." She stopped me on my way back and nudged me into a chair.

I cringed and stared at the tabletop. Here goes. Mom told her about the envelope, and then there was a long pause. I split a cookie and nibbled at the sugary filling.

"Wha—you what?" I raised my eyes at the surprised tone in her voice. Mom's eyes danced back and forth between the envelope and me: up, down. Up, down. A short laugh, like a bark, escaped her lips. I put my cookie down. Through the receiver, I could hear Aunt Doreen's high-pitched voice staccatoing through the conversation.

Mom's eyes bounced back to me. She covered the receiver with a hand. *Her,* she mouthed.

Huh? I mimicked Mom's Questioning Eyebrows from earlier.

She did it, with a gesture toward the receiver. "I can't believe you didn't tell me," she said out loud.

Of course! It hit me like Ben's unlucky fly ball. Aunt Doreen was the one who submitted my picture. Aunt Doreen! Instead of responding I stuffed my mouth with a whole cookie.

In the next few minutes, Mom and Aunt Doreen worked out exactly what I should wear for each section of the contest, discussed what would happen when I won, and how it would change my life and theirs. Through the whole thing, I sat at the kitchen table, the Prisoner of the One-Sided Conversation, working my way through a row of Oreos. I stacked the discarded tops and then licked away the sugary filling. Tops and bottoms were eaten last. Each time I tried to flee, Mom's hand clamped over the receiver and she'd hiss, "Just *wait*. This is so exciting!" When I tried to stand, she actually snagged my elbow and pulled me down again. The worst was when she thrust the phone at me.

"Hi, Aunt—" I never stood a chance of finishing.

"I can't believe it, Celeste! I mean, of course I do, but it's so *won*-der-ful. When we saw that ad I thought it would be perfect for Kirsten, but it's just so great that they liked your look and it's your shape that they want. There are so many opportunities for you. I just *had* to send in your school picture and that one from Christmas!" Her shrillness made my ears ring. I closed my eyes.

"Uh-huh, hmmm," I said. I opened my eyes to plead with Mom for rescue. She was too busy looking at the HuskyPeach catalog spread to notice. I concentrated on sweeping the scattered pile of crumbs in front of me into a straight line.

"You must be so excited you don't know where to begin. I

remember when Kathleen did her pageants; it takes time to get used to the idea."

She really liked them, I reminded myself. She's also a size four on a fat day. I haven't worn a four since I *was* four. My stomach somersaulted. *People are going to be looking at my picture. At me. Onstage. Wearing clothes for chubby teens. And Lively will find out.* I nearly choked at the thought. Her current taunts and comments would sound as nice as Theo Christmas's voice compared to what she'd come up with if I were a HuskyPeach model.

That couldn't happen. "Okay, Auntie. I'm going to give you back to Mom so I can, uhh, enjoy this moment." I slid the receiver across the table and left the two of them to finish planning my future.

Instead of enjoying anything, I went upstairs to figure out how I was going to end my modeling career before it began. Ben was sitting on the floor in the hall outside our bedrooms, cleaning gunk from his cleats. The doctor said he couldn't play baseball for two weeks after his concussion, but when that time was up, he'd be ready to do more damage in the name of outfielding. I stepped over his legs, splayed on the hall rug, and around the stinky shoes. I grasped the bedroom doorknob and paused to catch my breath from the trip up the stairs.

"Most people say hi when they get home from school." His eyes stayed focused on his cleats.

"Hi." I waited a beat. "Okay?"

He shrugged. "What was in that envelope? Mom was acting like it was a million dollars or something. She wouldn't open it, though. She was waiting for you." He raised his eyes to me.

With all of Ben's bumps, breaks, and bruises, you'd think he would look lumpy and weird, like that hunchback guy. Little kids must heal really well, because you couldn't tell he'd broken anything. His dark blond hair hung in his eyes, his nose—busted twice—was still straight, and his green eyes matched the specks in Mom's. In a kind of gross brother-way, he was a cute kid. Cutest, to tell the truth, when he was bandaged or in a cast. Maybe *he* should be the model.

"Nothing, really." I twisted the doorknob. "Just some stupid modeling thing that Aunt Doreen signed me up for. I don't even want to do it."

He tilted his head like he was listening to something far away. "Modeling, like they take your picture and stuff?" He waited for me to nod. "Yeah, you probably don't want to do it." He went back to scraping the bottom of a shoe.

"What's that supposed to mean," I asked. "Why wouldn't I? I could be a model." I stood straight and smoothed my sweatshirt over my tummy, annoyed that my eight-year-old brother felt so sure that I wouldn't be interested. And that he was right.

Ben stopped scraping, setting the shoe beside him on the hall floor, and ticked the reasons off on his fingers. "You don't like having your picture taken, you hate going shopping, and Aunt Doreen made you do it."

Bull's-eye. I slouched again. "If it's so obvious to you, why doesn't Mom realize it?" I jiggled the knob in frustration.

"Dunno." He shrugged. "Maybe she's hoping you'll change your mind."

She'd better have a lot of hope. "Maybe." I gave the doorknob a final twist and went into my room to take refuge in Theo.

During dinner Mom couldn't stop talking about my new career to Dad and Ben (I finally stopped protesting that I was too young to hold a part-time job, never mind Begin A Career).

"I didn't even enter the contest," I said at one point. "Aunt Doreen did. Shouldn't she be doing this instead of me?"

Mom scowled. "That is not a very nice thing to say, Celeste. You might not appreciate what she did for you now, but when you get older, you'll realize how important this moment is."

Doubt it, I thought, but I knew better than to say any more.

"Besides," Dad said, patting his belly, "it's about time that people recognize that being something other than a stick figure is beautiful. No offense, dear," he added to Mom.

Easy for you to say—you don't have to be the "big is beautiful" poster child.

I spent the rest of dinner trying to tune them out and wishing that I could talk to Sandra. She had an evening meeting for her traveling soccer team, and her parents wouldn't let her use the phone or computer until her homework was done. So I went to my room in search of solace.

Just me and you tonight, I said to Theo. Unfortunately, he didn't have much to say about the HuskyPeach.

You're great just being you, he told me.

"Wish everyone else felt that way," I muttered in response.

Chapter 6

"MOOOVE IT, SPEW!" A book corner scraped my shoulder as I was shoved to the side of the hall. "No cows allowed!" The day after my Yurk Fest was proving to be a Celeste-Taunting Lively Bonanza. Her hair swung past before I could think of a response.

I slumped into a seat in Mrs. O'Brien's Language Arts class. Beside me, Sandra doodled on her notebook. It was the first time I'd seen her all morning.

"Hey," she said. "How're you feeling?"

For a minute, I thought she was talking about the HuskyPeach. Then I remembered.

"Fine, but something else—" The tardy bell cut me off, and as it finished, Lively slid into the room. Language Arts was the one class where we didn't have assigned seating, and the only unoccupied desk was behind me. *Great.*

"Take a seat, Ms. Carson," Mrs. O'Brien directed.

Lively strutted down our row and thumped into the chair

behind me. Mrs. O'Brien started talking about the theme of power in *The Lord of the Flies*.

"Hey! Sandra!" Lively hissed. I hunched my shoulders at the sound. *What did she want Sandra for, anyway?* Sandra never talked during class, so I expected Lively to tire herself out whispering.

"Ms. Carson? You seem interested in talking today."

I stared straight ahead, trying not to be seen. Lively didn't respond.

"My answer?" Mrs. O'Brien said.

"Can you repeat the question?" Lively used a sweet voice. Mrs. O'Brien was about Language Arts, not sweetness. Behind her glasses, her eyes narrowed.

"You heard me. Or should have. Conch shell. Significance." She made a "come on" gesture with one hand.

"Oh. Yeah." I could tell Lively was stalling. "Urm, Celeste and I were just talking about that this morning, actually. Right, Celeste?"

I don't know who was more surprised, Mrs. O'Brien, the rest of the class, or me. My classmates' eyes slid in my direction, waiting to see how I'd respond.

"You were?" Mrs. O asked.

No! I shouted in my head. What came out was, "Well, not exactly . . ."

Mrs. O'Brien stepped toward our seats. "Ms. Carson, I'm afraid Ms. Harris seems to have forgotten your conversation. Please enlighten her and the rest of us as to the conch shell's significance."

Embarrassment and anger were coming off Lively in

waves. *Gotcha,* I thought, even though I knew I'd have to pay for this moment eventually.

"The sea?" Lively said, voice tentative.

"The sea?" Mrs. O'Brien repeated. "Really?" Two rows over, Philip Mikowski let out a low chuckle. O'Brien went in for the kill.

"Well, that's where it *came* from," Lively replied, a defiant tone creeping into her voice. "And they're on an *island,*" she finished. I clenched my teeth to stifle a smile.

"Ah-haa," Mrs. O'Brien replied. "Ms. Harris, do you have anything to add about the conch shell? Or the sea?" She wore her Expectant Expression.

Language Arts was one of my favorite subjects, and Mrs. O'Brien knew I knew the answer. *But don't drag me into this!* I tried to plead with her using my eyes. She would wait me out, I knew it.

"Power," I said, the word coming out as a croak. I cleared my throat. "The conch shell gives the power to speak to whomever has it."

"Whoever," she corrected.

I swore I could feel Lively's irritation on the back of my neck.

Satisfied with my answer and more concerned with note-passing on the other side of the classroom, Mrs. O moved on.

Lively waited a few minutes, then hissed Sandra's name again.

"What?" Sandra breathed. So much for not talking. I sneaked a peek at her: eyes locked on Mrs. O'Brien, hissing

out of one corner of her mouth, poised like she was taking notes—Sandra looked like a class-chatting pro, not like my honors-student straitlaced best friend.

"You play soccer?" Lively was speaking at nearly full volume, seeming to not care if she was heard again.

Why is Lively asking stupid questions? Everyone knew that Sandra played soccer. She got awards at assembly every year.

Sandra nodded. "Mmmm."

"I just signed up for Kick Off tryouts," Lively said. Mrs. O'Brien shot a stern look in our direction.

Sandra sat straighter. That was her traveling squad. I twisted to the side so I could see better.

"Ms. Harris, face forward," O'Brien barked. Sandra dropped her head and my face heated up. I received a sharp poke in my back.

"Don't moooove," Lively hissed.

"Knock it off," I muttered.

"Oooh, make me," Lively taunted. I looked to Sandra, buried in *The Lord of the Flies* so deeply it looked as though the spine had been surgically attached to her nose.

"Cut it out, Lively," Sandra hissed from between the pages.

Lively resumed her conversation as though Sandra hadn't spoken. "So I'm trying out and I want some extra help. I thought you could talk to me about it at lunch."

At *lunch?* Sandra and Millie ate with me every day except Thursdays, when they had class council meetings. That's when I got extra help in algebra from Dr. Mastis. Some weeks

I didn't need as much tutoring as others, but I'd rather eat with him and discuss x than sit by myself in the caf. It's a decent system. Katy goes to the high school early to work on chem labs, so she's never around.

Sandra rolled her eyes. "I don't think so," she said. I smiled at Sandra. *Take that, Lively!*

"Oh," Lively said, like she was hurt. She waited a second, then spoke again. "That's too bad. Robbie Flan said you are the person to ask."

The Lord of the Flies was still propped in front of Sandra's nose. "Robbie said that?" came her muffled whisper.

"Uh-huh. He sits with me a lot. Says a lot of things about you, actually." Lively's voice oozed sticky charm. *Don't fall for it!* I shouted in my head. *She's lying!*

Sandra's voice warmed. "Really? Like what?"

"Oh . . . stuff," Lively responded. "Sit with me today and we can talk about it. *After* you tell me about tryouts." It was like listening to a snake charmer. She was hypnotizing my best friend.

Sandra fell for it. "Okay."

My stomach shriveled, then rolled around the hollow place it left in my gut. I tried to glare at Sandra out of the corner of my eye, but it's hard to glare sideways. Sandra knew I couldn't stand Lively, and she heard all the garbage Lively said to me. I couldn't help but think, once Robbie's name comes up, Sandra gets amnesia. A bitter taste filled my mouth. My desire to tell her about the HuskyPeach withered.

For the rest of the class period, I couldn't concentrate.

Lively and Sandra didn't talk any more, but it didn't matter. Not talking was almost worse—it was like they shared a secret that they didn't want me to know about. Worst of all was Sandra's refusal to look in my direction. The bonus Bad Moments in Language Arts? Mrs. O'Brien called on me two more times and both times I had to ask her to repeat the question. Each time, Lively snickered.

When the bell to end the period finally rang, I stuffed my books into my bag.

"Hey," I said to Sandra, who also was putting her stuff away.

"Huh?" she said.

Before I could get another word out, a certain ponytail popped into my vision. "Sandra, don't you have social studies next? Let's walk over to H-wing." Lively parked herself directly in front of my seat, preventing me from getting out of my chair and blocking my view of Sandra.

I clenched the straps of my bag in frustration. "Hey, Sandra, I—" I started.

Lively tossed her head toward me. "No one can hear you." She slid between the chairs in the row and headed toward the door. Sandra glared at her, clacking a Jolly Rancher against her teeth. Behind her, kids were filing in for O'Brien's next class.

"She's tricking you!" I hissed.

"She's just being—" she began.

"Sandra," Lively barked from the door. "The late bell is going to ring! We can catch Robbie before his next class."

"A jerk?" I finished.

Sandra raised her eyebrows and shoulders in my direction, then turned toward the door—and Lively. A piece of lead dropped into my middle from somewhere in my chest.

"I just want to talk to Robbie," Sandra whispered over her shoulder.

"Ms. Harris," Mrs. O'Brien asked, "will you be staying for a second class?"

Face burning, I gathered my bag and bumped my way around the kids settling into their seats.

"Watch it, Wide Load," Philip Mikowski jeered as I bumped into his backpack. The tardy bell rang when I reached the hall. I leaned against the wall and let hot tears fall.

After fourth period, I found Sandra at her locker.

"It's only one lunch," she apologized. "Robbie Flan does sit with Lively sometimes," she said, a glint of excitement in her eye. "It'll just be this one time. And Millie will be there, so you guys can eat together." She clicked a Jolly Rancher against her teeth. "Look, I'll call you tonight and tell you all the stupid things they say," she promised, and left me at the door of the caf—jilted, angry, and wishing for an Emergency Twinkie from my locker stash.

Millie had a lunchtime orthodontist appointment, so I sat alone, in a corner. I tried not to notice Sandra devouring her pimento loaf sandwich (her favorite) smack in the middle of Lively's table, like she was part of the Ponytail Brigade. Once or twice I saw Sandra glancing in my direction, but every time she tried to get out of her chair Lively grabbed her arm

49

and they started laughing about something. I forced down only half of one of my peanut butter and jelly sandwiches (my favorite) and went to science early. At least there, I couldn't hear Lively's and Sandra's giggles. The distance helped soothe the aching around my heart.

Between afternoon classes I found Sandra in the hall.

"It was nothing," she said. "No big deal."

If it was no big deal, why wouldn't she look me in the eye?

Chapter 7

SANDRA WON'T BECOME *friends with Lively,* I kept telling myself as I trudged home from school that afternoon. *She knows what a sneaky weasel Lively is.* In fact, in fifth grade Lively had left a wet painting on a chair in the art room, and started calling Sandra "diarrhea pants" when she accidentally sat on it. *Okay, she knows Lively's not all sugar and spice. Then why is she helping her with soccer tryouts?* I finally hit on the reason: *She's setting her up, just like in* Lord of the Flies. *She only wants Lively to think she's being friendly, then she'll turn the tables on her.* Almost satisfied, I was sure Sandra would tell me the details about her Secret Plot to Destroy Lively during our nightly phone call . . . But the tightness in my stomach wouldn't go away.

After dinner, I went back up to my room to start my homework and wait to hear from Sandra. My need to talk to her about the HuskyPeach had returned, but I didn't know how to bring it up.

I tried addressing Theo for practice: "Hi, I might be a model." Then, "Hey, guess what, my parents want me to go to San Francisco in two weeks for a professional photo shoot." According to Theo's reaction, either of those approaches sounded good. I knew better. Even if Theo could like me for who I was, putting the words "plus-sized" in front of the word "model" changed everything. It was so embarrassing. "I'm going to be a fat girl model" and "I'm in a chubby girl modeling contest," sounded even worse. The whole situation was a cruel joke. Most people would be excited about the possibility of being a model—the glamour, the clothes, the cool parties, and doing fun stuff for magazine shoots. Everything about it should be fairy tale sweet, Hollywood cool. In place of Hollywood glamour, I got a bad sitcom. Instead of knights in shining armor, my fairy tale was filled with wormy apples. Theo Christmas watched me with sympathy, a Prince Charming with a guitar instead of a steed.

By eight thirty, I still hadn't heard from Sandra. We called each other every night no later than eight fifteen, unless our families were away. She called me Mondays and Wednesdays; I called her on Tuesdays and Thursdays. I double-checked my calendar: Wednesday. *Maybe her family went out to dinner,* I thought. *Maybe they're late getting back.* But that couldn't be true. Sandra's Grammie Jean, who lived with them, had to take medication every night at eight, so Sandra's family never stayed out late.

Eight thirty-six. My stomach felt like a tangled ball of

yarn. *Just call. You do it every other school night.* I stared at the phone receiver, willing it to ring. *Just call.* I wanted to hear all about the Secret Plot to Destroy Lively. I wanted to believe there was one. If I didn't pick up the phone, I could imagine what Sandra and I would talk about—how great it would be to laugh at what Lively and her lame friends said at lunch.

Eight forty-two. The imaginary conversations weren't interesting anymore. Before I could give it much thought, I picked up the phone with slick hands and punched her number. The purr of the ring tickled my ear. One . . . two . . . three . . . The McGees' voice mail picked up on the fourth ring when they weren't home. A click.

"Hello?" Slurp, smack. It was Sandra.

"Hey," I said, swallowing what felt like an entire Jolly Rancher.

"Celeste? Wait—what day is it? Is it Thursday?" The candy clicked against her teeth.

"Uhh, no. Wednesday. But it was getting late, and I . . ." I couldn't think of what to say.

"Oh no! I totally lost track of time. Umm, well, I'm on the other line. Can I call you after?"

Sandra knew my parents don't like the phone to ring after nine. *And who was she on the other line with, anyway?* Part of me knew. Really knew. "That's okay. We'll talk tomorrow," I said, staring up at my bedroom ceiling.

"Sorry. Okay, then," she said. "I should get back. Um, Lively is going to her first Kick Off tryout tomorrow and I'm just trying to give her an idea what to expect. It's no big deal."

"Sure," I said, blinking. "No big deal."

"And guess what?" She went on without waiting for my answer. "She told me a new way to pull my hair back that'll make my eyes look bigger. *And* she thinks that Robbie Flan might have been looking at me in science today!"

"Great," I responded.

After Sandra clicked back to Lively's call, I sat with the receiver to my ear, hoping she'd change her mind, and hoping the deep, throbbing pain in my middle would go away. But you can only take so much silence.

I dropped the phone onto my green comforter. To distract myself, I picked up the PeachFest Modeling Challenge itinerary and gave it a closer look. After dinner, Mom insisted that I bring it upstairs so I could get used to the idea. The first event was an interview and photo shoot at the company's headquarters. *PeachWear models*, the insert said, *are girls who are both engaging personalities and beauties. The interview process is designed for you to show us your sparkly, bubbly you! It's our goal to have the HuskyPeach represented by girls who are willing to take a bite out of life and savor every moment.* Wrinkling my nose, I thought, *Life's not all we "Husky Peaches" take bites out of.* Attached was a card that I had to return to confirm my candidacy for the contest.

According to the PeachFest Modeling Challenge Time-Line, the interview and photo shoot would take place a week from Saturday, then the other two events would be spaced out over four weeks. The PeachWear Spring Fling San Francisco Fashion Extravaganza was scheduled for May

19. There was something significant about that date, but my brain wasn't making connections—probably because the perfumed paper was making my eyes water.

I could just not go, I thought. *Refuse.* Really, what could Mom and Dad do? Make me? Force me to sit through the interview? Ground me until I agreed to be in a fashion show? Besides, there was no way I would win. To prove it, I slid off the bed and stood in front of the mirror over my dresser.

Flat brown hair, brown eyes, light skin. There wasn't anything unique or distinctive about my features: straight nose, round lips. Definitely *not* model material. I stepped back for a wider view. *Especially* not model material: round, round, round. Moon-shaped face, a round body, and a belly that pushed at the front of my shirts and pants when I was forced to wear something other than my track pants—and I owned a few pairs that had gotten snug. *Models* had skinny bodies, big boobs, and gorgeous eyes and hair. Models' thighs did not rub together when they walked, models did not get out of breath when climbing stairs, and models *absolutely* did not throw up on their gym teacher's shoes after chugging diet drinks.

" 'Spew' is right," I muttered. Oh yeah: And a model's best friend did not ditch her to talk to Lively Carson. No matter what Lively said about Robbie Flan. I'd had enough of the mirror, so I tugged on my pajamas without glancing at my reflection or my body and sat on the bed.

How could Aunt Doreen do this to me? Just because

Kathleen was in pageants, and Kirsten wouldn't/couldn't do it, why was I next in line? And what were these Peach-people thinking when they saw my pictures? They must not have gotten a lot of entries.

Between my New Career, New Nickname, and Best Friend's New Friend, this was shaping up to be a winner of a day. The shred of hope that there was a Secret Plot to Destroy Lively was small, but I held on as tightly to that as my mother did to the idea that I could win the Modeling Challenge.

Chapter 8

"STOP PULLING AT it," Mom said. "You'll stretch the fabric."

I scowled. "It's too tight." I tugged at the front of the blue shirt she'd forced me to try on. We'd been at the mall for nearly two hours trying to find something for me to wear to Kathleen's rehearsal dinner. So far, I'd been subjected to sausage-shaped dresses, bubble skirts, and a couple pair of shapeless pants. Nothing fit right, looked right, or was the right length for my stubby legs. It was hard to tell who was more exasperated, Mom or me.

"It looks *nice* on you," she tried. "You can't see it from my perspective. It shows your shape and is so much better than those awful sweatshirts. Go look in the mirror."

"I don't like it," I said. "I'm not comfortable." The pile of discarded clothes in the dressing room was large enough to lose a small child in. *I might've tried on everything in the store,* I thought. Nothing felt as good as my hoodie and track pants.

Everything was Not-Celeste—trying too hard and doing too little with too much.

Mom threw her hands up. "Fine. We're done here," she said. "We've both been tortured enough for one day. Get dressed." She must have seen the relief spread across my face, because she added, "*You* can tell your aunt that you have nothing to wear to your cousin's rehearsal dinner."

"The wedding isn't for seven weeks," I said, closing the dressing room door. I wriggled out of the blue shirt.

"Oh good. More shopping," she said from the other side. Back in my typical uniform, I followed her out of the store, wondering which of us would cave in first next time.

"We won't be much longer," Mom said, navigating the flow of fellow shoppers. "I just want to find a treat for Ben—something to cheer him up while he gets over his concussion. And we need to get Coach Anapoli's shoes."

I groaned. After finding out about my Yurk Geyser trick, Mom wanted me to give Coach Anapoli a new pair of sneakers to apologize.

"We don't even know her size," I said, trying to distract her and hurrying to keep up with her pace. The only thing more embarrassing than throwing up on a teacher's shoes, I was convinced, was bringing said teacher a new pair to replace the ones that had been, um, soiled.

My comment made her pause. "Good point," she said, giving me a curt nod. "We'll just get her a gift card so she can pick them out herself."

I gave up.

We reached the Catch 'N' Kick. Mom beelined for the baseball stuff and I leaned against a big bin of tennis balls to wait. To occupy myself, under my breath I sang along with the mall-music version of Theo Christmas's "Last Night" being pumped through the store's speakers. In my head, Theo was complimenting my version, asking me if I wanted to sing a duet with him.

"Hey Celeste."

Startled, I spun to see the voice's owner. Geoff, Sandra's brother.

"Hey," I said. I could feel my cheeks turning pink. Geoff and Kirsten went to high school together, and even though I'd known him as long as I'd known Sandra, it wasn't like I was one of his friends or anything. He was nice—he'd say hi when I was hanging out with Sandra at the McGees'—but that was the extent of our interaction. However, his dark eyes and sandy hair, plus strong shoulders and friendly attitude, made him the object of desire of the entire sophomore class. And then some.

"What're you doing here?" he asked.

"Getting something for my brother," I said. He kept watching me, and I didn't know what else to say. "What are you getting?"

"Paid," he said, and laughed. My face burned. I hadn't noticed his green polo shirt, whistle, and name tag. Behind him, at the store entrance, I spotted a collection of blond ponytails hovering around a display. Giggles floated in our direction.

"Oh." "Last Night" ended, and a pop song I didn't recognize took its place.

Geoff smiled, flashing dimples. "It's okay. I just started last week."

"All set," Mom said, saving me from having to think of another response. She clutched a green Catch 'N' Kick bag. "Ben's got a new glove, and Coach Anapoli can have her pick of sneakers."

Before Geoff could ask the question displayed on his face, Mom continued.

"Hi, Geoff," she said. "You work here now?" He nodded. The blond group was still at the front of the store. The giggles got louder, and I stopped paying attention to Mom and Geoff's conversation. One ponytail separated itself from the rest and bopped its way through the racks of sports gear, headed straight for us. As it moved from behind a display, I saw that the ponytail was attached to Carlee Morgenstern, Former Hair Experimenter. *Guess she learned her style lesson,* I thought. Her face glowed with terror or excitement, or maybe a mix of both. She saw me and paused, then took small, jerky steps in our direction again. *If Carlee's here, Lively's here.* My stomach tightened.

Mom and Geoff were peering into the bag at the glove.

"That's a good one," Geoff said, nodding. Carlee stepped closer.

"Um," she said, in a voice so low I could barely hear her.

Geoff was explaining the virtues of glove stitching.

Carlee cleared her throat. "Um," she tried again, a little louder.

This time Geoff glanced up. When he turned to her, Carlee froze.

"Can I help you?" he asked, when it became obvious that she wasn't going to do anything but stand there. The blond ponytails at the front of the store went silent.

"Um," she tried, and glanced back from where she came. "Um, someone over there needs help?" she said, raising the last word as though asking a question.

Geoff's eyes darted in the direction of the blondes. When he saw the group, he rolled his eyes. "Be right there," he mumbled to Carlee. She scampered back to the herd. Squeals ensued.

"Duty calls," Mom said. "Thanks for the information about the glove. Ben will be thrilled."

Geoff nodded. "He'll like it. See ya," he directed at me as he went to help his next customers.

Mom and I trailed behind, and by the time we reached the front of the store, Geoff stood in the center of a Ponytail Circle, describing different types of soccer cleats on a rack to the now-attentive group. I caught Lively's glare—and her perfect lips mouthing the words *solar eclipse* in my direction. I stared at the ground. I didn't need to see any more.

Chapter 9

TWO DAYS LATER, the solution to my Peachy problem presented itself in, of all places, gym class. Coach Anapoli instructed us to sit in the shower area. Light brown stains splotched her sneakers. The apology gift card was still stuffed deep in my backpack; I hadn't figured out what to say when I gave it to her.

"We are adding new curriculum this year," she said, twirling her whistle. "Since you girls are getting older, and the science classes have to deal with getting you ready for standardized tests, we had to make some changes to what we usually do in gym."

"Oh God," murmured Sandra, sitting in front of me, "please, please, *please* don't let it be sex ed."

Next to me, Katy and Millie shuddered.

Coach cleared her throat to silence the whispers that echoed off the tiles. "We are going to begin a classroom-based unit on nutrition," she stated. "For two weeks, alternating with soccer sessions, we will examine what we eat and how food affects our bodies." A ripple of relief, almost as visible as a sporting arena wave, swept through the room. Then, as Coach Anapoli began explaining about our food logs and materials, it came to me: *I could go on a diet.*

Right, I know—like this had never occurred to me before. Truthfully, until starting AlHo as a sixth grader, I'd never even thought about my weight. In elementary school, there was plenty of other stuff to worry about—what to bring for lunch, a do-it-yourself haircut gone wrong, accidentally calling the teacher "Mom"—just getting the hang of school was hard enough. And once I started AlHo, I stayed focused on what mattered—doing well and getting through the day. The Diet Drink of Horror had been my first—and most definitely my *last*—attempt at magic weight loss.

If I lose weight, I can't be a HuskyPeach, I reasoned. The irony was striking: I'd be too thin to be a model. I made sure to take a copy of each of the handouts Coach sent around the room, then tuned her voice out as I examined the USDA Food Guide Pyramid brochure.

"Hey," the snide voice interrupted my planning. "Dreaming about your next meal? Class is over." The blond ponytail bounced out of the showers.

"She shouldn't be saying that," said a soft voice to my left. Sandra stood, hugging her books, shaking her head at Lively. "She's really not like that when—"

"When you're spending hours on the phone together," I finished. "Yeah, I'm sure she's great."

"*San*-dy!" Lively sang from around the corner. "Let's go-oh."

"Sandy?" I repeated. Sandra hated to be called Sandy.

Sandra gave me a small smile and shrugged. "She likes it. She also told me that Robbie might sit with her at lunch this week. Do you think he will?" "Sandy" hustled out of the locker room to catch up without waiting for my response.

I brought the now-familiar hurt to my locker, where I'd stashed my bag at the beginning of class. Katy and Millie perched on the bench between the rows, waiting for me.

"What's up with her?" Millie asked, wrapping a lock of her thick, dark hair around her finger. She was wearing her "Fabulous & Filipino" pink hoodie as her Favorite Color Item of the Day. For some reason, people think she's quieter than she is. Maybe because she's short? In reality, she's got this loud laugh and makes a lot of jokes. It surprises people. But there was no hint of a joke in her question about Lively.

"She always says stuff like that." I shrugged and bent to twist my combination into the lock.

"Not Lively," Katy explained. "Sandra. She's been following Lively around like a puppy." Logical and thoughtful, Katy uses her science brain for problems outside the classroom too. She observes how people act and treat one another, then makes predictions about how they'll behave in the future—like when our seventh-grade English teacher's eye started doing this funny twitch in class, Katy kept saying that teaching wasn't for her and she was heading for a meltdown. One day, she left after second-period break and never came back. Unfortunately, I didn't need much logic to predict my best friend's behavior these days.

I tugged my bag out and straightened. "I don't know," I said, and slid the nutrition handouts into the front pocket, taking care not to rumple them. We started toward the door. "Ever since Lively went to tryouts for her soccer team, Sandra's been saying how nice she is. And how close she is to Robbie Flan."

"She's never nice to *you*," Millie pointed out, "and Robbie's kind of a jerk."

"Mm-hmm," I said. *Tell me something I don't know, okay?*

"What does Sandra say about it?"

How could I tell Millie that Sandra didn't *say* anything about it? That she barely called last week? That every time I called *her*, she rushed through our conversation and didn't seem to notice that all we talked about was homework? Or Robbie Flan, and what Lively *thought* he *might* have said or done? That I hadn't seen her out of school lately because Lively's mom always picked them up after practice and took them for ice cream? That at night, the loneliness was getting so bad that I did extra-credit homework assignments so I wouldn't have to think about Sandra? That I was pretty sure I was losing my best friend to my worst enemy?

"Look," Katy said as we stopped in front of the main hall, saving me from answering, "we'll talk about this more tomorrow. I've gotta study for my afternoon chem test on my way to the orthodontist. My mom's outside."

We wished her luck, and Millie promised to call that night to see how it went. Katy and Millie had been best friends forever. They went to the same nursery school and were in their elementary school Gifted and Talented program together. Sandra and I got to know them our first year at AlHo. The warning bell buzzed.

"See you," Millie said, turning toward the math wing and ending our conversation. Relieved, I waved and went to algebra.

Concentration was hard to come by in the rest of my morning classes. I kept thinking of the food log and nutrition guide in my backpack. *That's it,* I thought. *Just lose enough weight so that they won't want me to be their model.* The plan seemed so easy. Carrot sticks. Pita bread. I thought of every diet food I'd ever seen advertised. I imagined the woman in the red bathing suit from the Diet Drink of Horror recipe, shaking her head, saying, "It's no good. She's too thin to be a HuskyPeach," in front of a panel of judges.

I couldn't wait to tell Sandra about my plan and the HuskyPeach at lunch, but when I met her at her locker she was excited about something else.

"Robbie Flan is going to sit at Lively's table *today,*" she said, bouncing on the balls of her feet with excitement. "She said I could sit with them too. Is that okay? 'Cause if you don't want me to, I won't." She stopped bouncing and her head drooped when she said that last part.

"Sure," I said, swallowing hard against the stab in my heart. "Go ahead. We'll talk later. I'll eat with Millie."

"I'll call you tonight and give you all the details. Promise," Sandra said, bounce back, and she was gone—along with my desire to tell her about my plans.

Later that afternoon, though, I'd regained my dieting enthusiasm. I barely even noticed when Lively knocked into me and mooed between math and science. I wanted to take out the nutrition information and read it, but I knew what would happen if I dared do it at school. So I waited. The rest of the day passed by as slowly as ketchup sliding from a full bottle.

When I finally got home, the house was empty. A note from Mom revealed that she'd taken Ben for his follow-up appointment for his concussion. Glad to have the quiet, I spread the nutrition information across the table. I read about calorie counts, sugar, fat, and protein, and examined the food log we were supposed to fill out. It was stuff I'd heard of before, of course—who hadn't?—but I'd never wanted to pay attention to it. Until now.

There were even sample healthy menus on some handouts and a height and weight chart to help calculate BMI—a ratio that showed how overweight you were. After following the calculations, once again I found myself in the "needs improvement" category. According to the handout, I needed to lose about twenty pounds to not be in the "unhealthy" weight range.

Twenty pounds. The number reverberated through my head like a gigantic echo. I didn't think I had to lose *that* much . . . but I wasn't about to step on a scale and get hard evidence one way or another. There was no way I could lose twenty pounds in six weeks. *But if I lose* some *weight,* I thought, *I still might be too thin to win.*

I flashed back to the Diet Drink of Horror. If only that had worked . . . but its rancid taste and belly-flipping effects left an impression that I wouldn't forget.

I tried optimism. *This won't be so bad.* Most of the stuff on the healthy food lists were things I liked—chicken, fruit, and vegetables. The key was eating smaller amounts of everything. And not eating cookies. That would be a little tougher, but it would just be for a couple of weeks, until I lost a few pounds. Starting right away would be best. Instead of my usual after-school snack of chocolate cookies and milk, I went to the fridge and pulled out an apple. And took one cookie out of the bag. Then I glanced at the apple in my other hand and put the cookie back. Sealed the bag. Reopened it and took two more.

This could be harder than I thought.

Mom and Ben came home with clearance for him to go back to baseball and a car full of groceries. Ben immediately ran upstairs to get his glove and banged out of the house to find someone to play catch with.

"Use your hands, not your head," Mom called after him, unpacking the bags. She shook her head. "Hopefully we won't have another incident for a couple of weeks. We need a break." She caught herself as I started laughing. "Oh, no! You know what I mean."

I began stacking canned goods in the pantry, still chuckling. "*Suuure.* You'll probably wish you'd never said that."

"You're right. But he needs to stay healthy until we can get you through the Challenge. Can't be trucking him around town to doctors when we have so much to do to get you ready too." She smiled a wide smile in my direction. Her words rained ice water on my good mood. I ducked deeper into the cabinet.

"Have you sent that card in yet?" *Maybe I could end this whole thing now.*

"Do you really think I should do this?" I said to the peas and corn.

"Do what?" Mom asked. "Honey, I can barely hear you. Come out of there."

I pulled my head out of the cabinet and straightened, then grabbed several soup cans from the counter and dove back in.

"You know, the Challenge thing. I mean, I'm still not sure if it's a good idea." I arranged the cans so the labels lined up perfectly. *Please, please don't make me do this. Don't make me interview, or do the photo shoot, or walk the runway. Or,* studying the new bag of Oreos on the top shelf, *diet.* I poked my head out.

"Honey, this really is a wonderful opportunity for you. You could get money for college. You'll learn so much. You could even get an agent and more modeling jobs. I wish you could see it from my perspective. You need to send in that form." She paused, one hand in the brown paper bag, and pushed a strand of hair behind her ear with the other.

Easy for you to say, I thought. With their "hummingbird metabolisms," Mom and Aunt Doreen were petite and pretty. My metabolism moved about as fast as a hippo's. So of course Mom'd be excited about a modeling opportunity. If I were a contestant in the SkinnyBanana Modeling Challenge, I'd be excited too.

"Your father and I want you to go through at least one session. Will you do that for us?" She turned to me.

"Just one?"

"It would mean so much and make us very, very proud." Her face was hopeful.

There it was, my way out, but I was too chicken to take it. Once she brought out the P-word, I was done for. I sort of half smiled and shook my head.

"Guess I'm just nervous," I mumbled. Giving the Oreos a wistful glance, I closed the pantry door. "Okay. One session."

Upstairs, I popped in a Theo Christmas CD and spread the HuskyPeach response card and nutrition handouts across my desk. *Chubby model or thinner, average person?* I thought. I glanced from one to the other. There was no way I wanted to be Miss HuskyPeach. *Why had I agreed to do this?*

While Theo sang, I opted to organize Operation Skinny Celeste. I would write down everything I ate over the next four weeks, sticking to the healthy food guides on the handouts. I dug out the food log, a brochure with a picture of a skinny cartoon girl holding an apple and a glass of milk on its cover, and studied the columns labeled *breakfast, lunch,* and *dinner* on the inside. There was a box at the bottom for snacks. *May as well start with today,* I thought, and listed what I'd eaten earlier as I sang along to "Dreaming Without You": "Now my nerves are shot, I have nothing to say . . . I know I've never felt this way."

Breakfast: bowl of cereal (Choco-Puffs), glass of orange juice. Lunch: 2 peanut butter and jelly sandwiches, small bag of chips (BBQ), chocolate chip cookie.

I jotted "Twinkies" in the snack box. And added the apple and two cookies I'd eaten downstairs. Easy enough. I could do this, no problem. It didn't even look like that much food, now that I'd written it down. No more HuskyPeach for me! The smile on my face was as bright as Theo's spotlight. I stuck my tongue out at the response card.

What about the candy from Dr. Mastis's desk? whispered a voice in my head. It was Red Bathing Suit Woman. *Didn't you take two pieces from his jar at the end of class?*

Thanks for the reminder, I replied, smile fading, and added them to my snacks list. That box looked pretty crowded.

And the soda you drank after lunch? she prodded. *You forgot that too.*

Of course. I listed it under the cookie. The smile dimmed even further. *Anything else?* I asked, annoyed with her smug tone. When she didn't respond, I put the pen down.

Didn't you get a granola bar from the vending machine before you left school? she asked. I imagined her smirking.

Didn't I squish you? I thought in reply. I scribbled the last item in the snacks box. There were no more lines left. *This could be more complicated than I thought,* I realized, reviewing my list. Only a few of the items I'd eaten all day were "healthy choices," according to the nutrition guide: the apple, the milk in the cereal, the sandwiches and the juice (which were kind of a stretch). Everything else was listed under "Food to

Be Eaten in Moderation." *We HuskyPeaches like to take bites out of life,* I thought. The response card mocked me.

"Celeste," Mom called from downstairs. "Come set the table."

Dinner.

Take smaller bites, Red Bathing Suit Woman suggested.

Chapter 10

"SINCE WHEN ARE you so interested in helping in the kitchen?" Mom asked as I helped her finish making the salad.

I shrugged, watching the water swirl down the drain as I rinsed the tomatoes. "Just thought it'd be nice," I offered. Once finished with my nightly chore, I usually made a break for it until dinner was on the table. But if Operation Skinny Celeste was going to work, I needed to be in the kitchen to make "healthy choices," according to my nutrition info. Especially when I packed my lunch. I blotted each tomato dry, then passed them to Mom for slicing and dicing. "What are we having, anyway?" I asked, enjoying a whiff of something yummy in the oven. It smelled familiar, but I couldn't place it.

"Homemade mac and cheese," Mom replied, scraping the tomatoes into the bowl of lettuce on the counter.

"Really?" My mouth watered. "What's the occasion?"

Mom only made mac and cheese for super-special dinners. The last time we had it was when Ben got the cast off his arm after breaking his wrist, and that was months ago.

"Oh, we have lots of things to celebrate these days," she said, handing me a cucumber and the vegetable peeler. I held the cuke over the sink and slid the peeler against its deep green skin. It came off in sheets, showing the white pulp underneath.

"Like what?" I asked, suspicious.

"Well, Ben being better, for one," she said. "And your exciting new opportunity. I even invited Aunt Doreen, Uncle Chuck, Kathleen, Paul, and Kirsten over to celebrate. You'll need to set extra places for them."

The last thing I wanted to do was celebrate my chubby model contestant-hood with anyone, let alone Aunt Doreen and company. Mom's words startled me, and I scraped a knuckle instead of the vegetable. "Ow!" I said. The peeler clattered into the sink. Drops of blood darkened the pile of shaved cucumber skin.

"Careful," Mom chided, turning the cold water on and holding my hand under the stream. "You are as dangerous to yourself in the kitchen as Ben is on the jungle gym." She smiled and rummaged through the junk drawer for a Band-Aid.

"Why'd you have to invite them over?" I struggled to unwrap the bandage and get it around my own finger. Mom, tired of watching me wrangle, came to my rescue.

"I invited them because they're family, and very excited for you," she said, her eyes darkening and brows dropping into her Stern Look. "And because without your aunt Doreen, you wouldn't have this opportunity." She gave my bandaged hand a gentle squeeze for reinforcement.

Pretty much, I agreed, but I didn't say anything. When Mom's back was turned, I slipped out of the kitchen. Plan or no plan, it was not the place for me.

When Aunt Doreen and Uncle Chuck got to our house, I was back in my bedroom, making an attempt at algebra homework. As a cruel reminder of the weight I needed to lose, every answer kept coming up as "negative twenty." Mom called me to come and say hi. I dragged my feet the whole way down.

"There she is!" Aunt Doreen squealed. "It's our little model!"

Little? Not quite. But I'm hoping to be too little to model, I thought. I held still while she squeezed bony hugs and pecked kisses on me. Hummingbird is right.

"There she is," Uncle Chuck boomed. He's the tallest person I've ever met, with big hands and long legs that match his loud voice. You'd think he'd be scary, but he just walks around behind Aunt Doreen, repeating what she says. She talks so much he never gets that many words out. He stooped to pat my back. "Our—what is it, Doreen? Healthy grape?"

"Husky peach," she murmured, studying me as though I had turned to gold.

"Our husky peach," he said. "Isn't that something? Where's Wes?" he asked my mom.

Mom directed him to the family room. All the while, Aunt Doreen cooed and clucked at me like I would break into pieces if I sneezed.

"Where are Kirsten, Kathleen, and Paul?" Mom asked.

"Kirsten had afternoon swim practice," Aunt Doreen replied, tearing her eyes away from me. "They're picking her up when she's done."

"Aunt Doreen made you something special, Celeste," Mom said. "You really didn't have to," she added, over my head.

"Oh?" *Please, please don't let it be what I think it is,* I thought, remembering my food log. For all of Aunt Doreen's messing in other people's business and nervous chatter, she is a great cook. And she makes the best—

"Butterscotch apple crumb cake."

"Great. Thank you, Auntie. It's my favorite dessert." Inside, I wilted. A warm slice of her crumb cake topped with creamy vanilla ice cream is like giving your belly a hug—it feels great and you want another one.

Operation Skinny Celeste encountered its first land mine. Negative Twenty was shaping up to be one rocky road.

Paul, Kathleen, and Kirsten arrived right before we ate. Kathleen is a taller, more beautiful version of Kirsten. They share the same long blond hair; however, Kathleen's eyes are clear green and her build would make Barbie jealous. But she doesn't make a big deal of it. She dresses in comfy clothes most of the time and never wears makeup. Paul, of course, is equally as good-looking—deep brown eyes, wavy hair, and a wide smile. Together, they resemble those plastic bride and grooms on top of wedding cakes.

"Hey, star," Paul said, giving me a peck on the cheek. I blushed.

"Not quite," I said.

"Well, I'm glad we booked you in our wedding party before you become a world-renowned model," Kathleen joked. She hugged me. Mom called us to eat, saving my face from melting from the heat of further teasing.

We squeezed around the table and enjoyed Mom's dinner. Thankfully, conversation focused on Ben's concussion. He recounted seeing the fly ball come at him as fast as a comet and jumping for it.

"Then I guess I got so excited that I forgot to bring my glove up to actually *catch* it," he finished, staring at his plate as his cheeks turned pink.

"It's okay," Paul said, with a rough pat on Ben's back. "Next time you won't."

Mom and Aunt Doreen cleared the dishes and brought out the butterscotch apple crumb cake, which had been warming in the oven during dinner. The sweet buttery smell filled the house. Dad placed a tub of vanilla ice cream on the corner of the table, and Mom sliced.

"Celeste should get the first piece," Aunt Doreen chirped from across the table. "After all, she's going to be fay-mous." Everyone turned to me.

I was sure my face turned darker pink than Ben's. "Ummm, thanks, Auntie. I don't know about that, though. I'll just have a little one," I said, thinking of Red Bathing

Suit Woman, Negative Twenty, and looking at my Living Barbie Cousins. "And"—I gulped—"no ice cream." I rushed the words out before I could change my mind.

"Come on," Uncle Chuck rumbled. "No ice cream?"

"Really?" Dad's eyes were wide. He gestured with the scooper. "Are you sure?"

I nodded, not trusting myself to speak. Mom passed a cake-topped plate to my dad and kept slicing.

"Celeste," Aunt Doreen cooed, leaning across the table like we were the only two in the room, "you don't have to worry about the Challenge. The HuskyPeach wants you just the way you are."

"Mom!" Kathleen said, shocked.

"I can't believe you just said that," said Kirsten. My ears were so hot, I was pretty sure they were on fire.

"Oh, honey, come on. Celeste is just nervous. You'll do fine, sweetheart," Aunt Doreen said, and patted my hand.

"You'll do fine," Uncle Chuck repeated. He dug into his brick-sized piece with a grin.

Falling into a hole in the floor would be fine *right about now,* I thought.

"Just a small piece for me too," Kirsten chimed in as Mom cut me a skimpy slice of cake and I tried to send a smile in Aunt Doreen's direction.

"I'm sure Celeste is just full. She'll have another slice later, right, honey? She always does. Sometimes more than one," Mom soothed. I stared at my plate.

Like fattening a pig, Red Bathing Suit Woman whispered in my head. Two weeks ago Aunt Doreen could barely look at me in the Monstrosity, and now she was concerned with increasing my cake consumption.

"There's that one plus-sized model who's pretty famous these days," Paul jumped in. "I can't remember her name . . . Daisy something? Rose someone? It's a flower. Anyway, she's big."

And this was supposed to make me feel better?

"What are you saying *that* for?" Kathleen glared at him with a stare that would rival her mother's.

"Huh?" Paul's face was covered in confusion. Then something clicked. "Oh. I didn't mean big like *big*. I meant big like . . . popular." He shoveled a piece of cake into his mouth, probably so he wouldn't say anything else to get him in trouble. The tips of his ears were pink.

Someone please give me my life back.

Bathing Suit Woman only chuckled.

After dessert, Kirsten, Kathleen, and I cleared the table while the moms looked at photos of bridesmaid bouquets for the wedding. Dad, Paul, and Uncle Chuck took Ben out to practice catching fly balls. When Ben ran upstairs to get his glove, he came back down with his football helmet too. "They're making me," he said with a shrug.

"Poor kid." Kathleen shook her head as she stood at the sink, rinsing plates. Kristen wrapped the leftover cake. "Gotta give him credit for trying, though."

I shuttled the plates to the dishwasher. "Uh-huh."

"So, are you psyched for this modeling thing, or what?" she said, turning to me. "You've barely said anything about it." She smiled.

At that second, with her perfect teeth and perfect hair and perfect skin and eyes focused on me, all that perfect helped me see how broken I was. I heard Lively's jeers, felt the ache of Sandra's continued rejections, and pictured the food log waiting for me upstairs while the Butterscotch Apple Crumb Cake of Temptation sat sentry on the kitchen counter. Negative Twenty never seemed so far away. Everything just rolled together and I couldn't help it, I started to cry. Tears slid off my face and onto the dishes in my hands, mingling with the watery streaks of ice cream and crumb cake.

"I—I—know," I blurted, unable to stop myself and mortified that I couldn't. My shoulders hitched as I tried to breathe, but stay quiet enough so Mom wouldn't hear. "I don't want to."

Kathleen stood frozen at the sink, like she'd stepped in dog poo and didn't want to check the bottom of her shoe. The tap gushed. She blinked.

"Wow, Celeste. It's okay." She turned the water off and grabbed a towel, then hustled across the kitchen, Kirsten following.

I struggled to stop, but couldn't. "I just—I just—" I scrunched my face in an effort to control myself. *How babyish is this?* I thought. Snot slid out of my nose, and I sniffed hard to suck it back in since I was still holding the plates and didn't have a free hand to grab a tissue. *So gross! They're my cousins and I'll have to live with this for the rest of my life.* Kirsten tugged the dishes from my grasp and set them on the counter.

Kathleen snagged a napkin from the holder and I took it gratefully, blotting my eyes and wiping my faucet-nose.

The tears slowed. She gave me a quick hug and stood back, hands on my arms, and looked down at me as I sniffled and hiccupped.

"You all right?" she asked, face serious.

I nodded.

"Really?"

"Think so," I managed, and sniffed again.

"Whoa," Kirsten said. She cleared a space on the counter and hoisted herself up. Kathleen leaned next to her. "What's the deal?"

Embarrassed by my snotty crying fit, I hung my head and studied my shoes. "Not much to tell."

"If you don't want to talk about it, that's cool," Kirsten said. She hopped off the counter and rinsed another plate. It was then that I realized I hadn't talked to *anyone* about it. I didn't have anyone to tell since Sandra was so busy with Lively. I stood there in stupid silence, listening to the water rush into the sink, pushing back the pain.

Kathleen loaded the dish into the dishwasher. She glanced in my direction.

"It's dumb," I tried. She nodded, encouraging me.

"It's just," I said again. "I don't want to be a HuskyPeach." The tears threatened to fall again, so I stopped.

She tucked her golden hair behind her ears. "Okay. So why are you doing it?"

My eyes returned to the floor, which I'd never studied so carefully. "Because my mom and dad and your mom are so excited about it. Because they think I can do it."

"But you don't?"

I shrugged. There were blue specks in the tile I never noticed. "I told Mom I'd do the first round, but now I don't know. What if people find *out*?"

It was her turn to shrug. "So?"

I knew what she was getting at—the whole "they're just jealous and that's why they'll make fun of it" theory—but that didn't work in this case. I seriously doubted there would be a lot of people at AlHo wishing they were walking that catwalk. And with Lively Carson stealing my best friend, I'd have to make my way alone. To go through with Miss HuskyPeach, I needed an ally—my own lieutenant, like Ralph in *The Lord of the Flies. And right now, there are a serious lack of candidates for the job.* But I couldn't say that either. So I gave her a half smile and tried to seem agreeable.

She saw right through it. "Look, I know. The whole thing stinks and people are mean. But if you do or don't do stuff because of what other people think, you'll end up wimpy, like a dishcloth." She waved hers for emphasis. Kirsten smiled in agreement.

"I guess," I said. Kathleen always did what she wanted and people listened to her. She probably never worried about being a Dishcloth Wimp.

"You're doing it because your mom wants you to, but you might get teased, so you don't want to. Figure out what *you* want and say the heck with them." She tossed the cloth over her shoulder and turned back to the sink.

"Not like that's easy either, but it's the only way you'll be happy. That's how I decided I didn't want to do pageants like Kathleen," Kirsten added.

I nodded, bringing my gaze from the floor to her. This time my smile was more genuine, but my insides were still shaky.

"I'll try," I promised, and gathered the dirty plates off the counter. *I need to figure out what I want first, though,* I thought. *And then deal with Mom.* As if reading my mind, Mom stuck her head in the room as I was bent over the dishwasher.

"Girls, are you done yet? Aunt Doreen and I want you to look at these bouquets, Kathleen."

"Be right there, Aunt Noelle," she responded. When I heard Mom's footsteps tapping in the direction of the family room, I straightened, relieved that she hadn't seen my blotchy face. More questions and tears were not what I needed.

Kathleen folded the dishcloth over the edge of a cabinet door to dry. "I'll see you out there," she said, and left.

Kirsten shook her head and rolled her eyes. "Flowers. How boring can you get?" She crossed the room, twisting her hair into a knot as she went.

"Kirsten," I said, my voice sounding weak to my own ears. She stopped, mid-knot, hands wrapped in loops of golden tresses, and turned in my direction with eyebrows raised.

"Thanks." Even though their words hadn't helped me that much, it was good to let it out—even if it *did* come out as a snot-filled mess.

She fiddled for a minute, and the knot sat snug on her head when she dropped her arms. "No problem." She took a few steps in the direction of the family room, then paused. "By the way, what's up with Sandra's new friend?"

"Huh?" I said, unable to make the Conversational Gear Shift.

"Sandra's friend. Geoff says she bugs him."

Lively. *Guess I'm not the only one she bugs*, I thought. I shrugged instead of answering and she left.

After washing my face and wiping down the counter, I was ready to face the Bouquet Bonanza. Leaving the room, the kitchen clock caught my attention: 9:15.

Sandra hadn't called.

Chapter 11

IN THE FOLLOWING days, Operation Skinny Celeste lumbered into motion. I avoided Twinkies, snacks, and chocolate cookies at all costs, but there were hidden minefields and snipers around every corner. First came the Butterscotch Apple Crumb Cake of Temptation, then there was the Brownie Pan Sneak Attack (Mom made them for Ben's class field trip to the planetarium and left some for me and Dad). That night, I found myself standing at the kitchen counter, staring at the brownies, while Dad was out playing catch with Ben, and Mom was at her desk.

Just one won't hurt, I thought, reaching out to the smallest one on the plate. The size of my school ID, it beckoned me with chocolaty delight.

Negative Twenty, hissed Red Bathing Suit Woman. *It'll become Negative Thirty if you aren't careful.* I scowled.

"Leave me alone," I whispered, trying to get her smug voice out of my head.

"Did you say something, honey?" Mom called.

I snatched my hand from the plate and spun around, guilty. Red Bathing Suit Woman chuckled.

"No."

Mom entered the kitchen, carrying a sheaf of papers for the trash. "I thought I heard you say something." When I shook my head, she left. "By the way," she called from her desk, "I mailed that card for you."

I'd been staring at the brownies again, not paying attention. *It really isn't a very big brownie,* I reasoned. *And it's homemade. That has to be better than store-bought cookies, right?*

"Card? What card?"

"For the Modeling Challenge," came her casual response. "It was on your desk when I was putting laundry away. I saw that you'd left it out, so I sent it in. We're all set for Saturday."

The brownie didn't look so appetizing after all. I was about to protest, tell Mom that she shouldn't have mailed it, when I realized that it was my fault for agreeing to do round one in the first place. My motivation for Negative Twenty reached the point of no turning back. I was a chubby modeling contestant. I had no choice but to lose weight—and the Challenge.

At the end of the week my resolve was put to the test. Typically, AlHo's cafeteria served up the usual hot lunch food: too-flat grilled cheese, suspicious pizza slices, and mystery meat tacos. But one Friday a term, the caf held barbecue day, or "BBQ day," as it said on the whiteboard menu by the hot lunch line. Everyone bought on BBQ days.

It was the one day I left my peanut butter and jelly home, choosing, instead, a hot dog and hamburger (because you can't pick just one) and a mountain of crinkle-cut golden french fries, which I smothered in ketchup. Never mind that real summertime barbecues didn't include fries as a side dish, at AlHo, BBQs always did. It was also the only day of the term that the caf served soda along with milk and juice.

But instead of soda, in front of me squatted a small carton of skim milk. In place of my burger or hot dog, a Tupperware container of spinach salad, with lemon juice for the dressing. And replacing french fries, for my dining pleasure, there was a small plastic bag of dry, white-tinged carrot sticks—no ridges, no crinkles, and no coating. I sighed. Seven days, and Operation Skinny Celeste was getting old. My pants didn't feel any looser, and I was still avoiding the scale. However, the first part of the Modeling Challenge, the interview and photo shoot, were the next day, so there was no way I giving up my plan for a fake BBQ. Even if I did love it. And want it.

At least Millie's getting a burger, I thought. *Maybe she'll share a fry or two.* I picked at my salad while I waited for her to come out of the line, trying not to stare at the passing lunch trays of BBQ goodness. I was also hoping this would be the day that Sandra sat with us for a full lunch period again. She'd taken to eating with Lively and coming over at the end to say hi. Each time, her visit sliced my heart like a paper cut. I didn't want to think about that. For distraction, I forced my thoughts to the new song I heard Theo Christmas was working on. How would it sound? Would it be as good as "Dreaming Without You," my current favorite?

Instead of daydreaming, I should've been paying attention.

"Oh look, the cow chews her cud!"

I swallowed quickly, nearly choking. Lively stood next to my table, balancing a tray of french fries with one hand, pointing with the other.

"Chew, chew!" Lively chanted, snickering. Her blue earrings and barrettes glinted like ice chips in the fluorescent lights.

Where's a lunch monitor when you need one? I thought.

My face felt huge and hot, as though the thin layer of skin was all that kept it from bursting. The cafeteria got quiet, all nearby eighth graders openly watching Lively torment me. Philip Mikowski and Robbie Flan, fresh from the lunch line, moved closer. Behind them, I could see Sandra, a puzzled expression on her face. She walked toward the table with slow steps, like weights were tied to her feet.

"What's the matter, cow, cat's got your tongue?" Lively said, and she caught sight of my drink. "Ooh, I see, you're a cow-nibal!" She snatched my skim milk carton. "The Skinny Cow," she read off the label. "You can't be serious. Trying to get skinny, cow?"

Now that she was close enough to hear Lively, I could see Sandra trying to edge away. I returned to my salad, fighting the fresh paper cut on my heart.

"Stop it," I mumbled, forcing breath from my chest, which felt like a cow was sitting on it. "Give it back." I couldn't bring myself to look up from the red and white checked tablecloth. I didn't want to see how my supposed best friend saw me. *This really can't be happening,* I kept telling myself, more concerned with Sandra's actions than Lively's words. *She is not just going to walk away while Lively does this to me.* But she never came to the table. The slice on my heart settled into a throb.

"What, cow?" Lively spit out the words in tight bursts, like cherry pits.

"Give it back. Give me my milk back." Instead of looking up, I studied my spinach salad. One of the pieces was soggy dark green around the edges.

"Make some more," Lively said, and turned to walk away. The boys hooted and mooed.

Heat rose in me like a volcano. *What tropical island tribe made her their queen?* I was sick of everything. Sick of being a dishcloth, sick of worrying about what I was eating, sick of waiting to lose Miss HuskyPeach, sick of listening to Lively's trash talk, and especially sick of watching Sandra follow Lively around like an adoring groupie.

The volcano in me erupted. "Give it back," I said, spewing hot lava, and said the worst word I could.

"You go, Tubby Tostada!" Someone—I think Robbie Flan—cackled.

Lively didn't miss a step. She turned her head and laughed.

"Nice try, fat girl." She tossed my milk carton in the nearest garbage can and never looked back.

All the heat generated by my anger disappeared, leaving

me feeling like a deflated balloon. I slumped in my seat, appetite gone, and wished I were living some other person's life.

"What the heck happened over here?" Millie arrived at the table. Not even her burger and fries were appealing after that exchange.

"Lively," I responded, some of my anger returning. "And Sandra. She walked away when Lively was—being Lively," I finished, unable to think of a way to describe the awful scene. I picked up my fork, poking the air with it as I spoke. "I can't believe she did that. I mean, she just *walked away.* Who does that to their best friend?" My face burned like it was on fire.

"Celeste," Millie said, her voice low, "Sandra hasn't been any kind of friend lately, let alone a best friend." She took a bite of her burger and waited for my response.

Millie was right. Sandra had stopped calling, wasn't interested in hanging out with me, and certainly wasn't interested in anything going on in my life, but I hadn't wanted to admit it. I was still hoping that the Secret Plot to Destroy Lively did, in fact, exist, but if it did, I was the only one plotting. Either that, or it was a *really* big secret. So big, and so secret, Sandra didn't know about it. That was highly unlikely.

"What do I do?" I said.

She swallowed. "Talk to her."

"Lively is in the only two classes we have together, Language Arts and gym, and gets in between us when I try. Like Sandra can't talk to me herself." I tapped my fork against the edge of the table. "I can't believe she did that," I said again. The volcano in me was rumbling, coming back to life. "I do have to talk to her."

Millie nodded, encouraging. She chomped a french fry in two.

"I need to know why she's being such a jerk to me. I haven't done anything to her."

She kept nodding, taking another bite of her burger.

"And we don't have any more classes together today." The fork clacked a quick beat.

"Yes," Millie said, her burger gone. "That's why you need to—"

"Go get her right now," I finished, dropping my fork and getting to my feet. Mount Celeste was ready to blow.

"That's not what I meant!" called Millie, but I barely heard her. I was already on my way to Lively's table.

Parked in the exact center of the caf, Lively's group of girls surrounded her like ants around a cookie crumb. *And ants can be stomped on,* I reminded myself. *And the crumb gets tossed.* All the girls—there were five or six of them—wore their hair in high ponytails and dressed in skirts that matched their shirts. They coordinated their barrettes and their earrings. *With those sparkling rhinestones and glittery jewelry, it's amazing that they're not blinded by the glare from their accessories.* The boys sitting at the table appeared mesmerized by the shiny fake jewels.

"I can't believe you did that," Carlee Morgenstern said to Lively. "I would've been terrified."

"No, you wouldn't have," Lively responded, shaking

her head. "It's about being confident. Thinking you can do anything, no matter what. You really could do it," she finished. After getting the advice, Carlee smiled like she'd just won a prize.

Some prize, I thought. *Lame advice from Lively.*

At first, I didn't spot Sandra. Her back was to me. As I got closer, though, I caught sight of her brown ponytail bobbing in the sea of blond. She was laughing about something, next to Robbie.

"Isn't that funny?" she said to him in a high, fake voice I'd never heard her use before. For some reason, that made me even angrier. *How can she laugh at anything when she was so mean to me?* I stopped behind Sandra's chair.

Robbie shrugged. "I don't get it," he muttered into his sandwich. *Couldn't she see that he didn't even like her?*

Conversation at the table dried up quicker than a puddle in the desert. Everyone's eyes turned to me.

"Sandra," I said, biting into her name like it was a crunchy french fry, "I need to talk to you."

Before she could even turn around, Lively broke in. "She doesn't talk to animals, cow. Shoo! Go back to your pen." Robbie laughed.

Evidently that's the stuff that he finds funny. Giggles swept around the table. Below me, Sandra's shoulders bunched around her ears.

I ignored the laughter. "Sandra."

"I *heard* you," she barked, in a gruff voice she'd never used with me. "Back up so I can get out."

My face, already hot, turned into a furnace. I stumbled

back a few steps. The pressure of anger leaked away. *Why did I think this was a good plan? What was I going to say to her? "Why won't you be my friend anymore?" "Why are you so mean to me?"* My heart hammered in fear. This conversation was turning into a Very Bad Idea.

"You're not talking to that cow, are you?" Lively said. Her mouth opened in a big, fake O of shock. "I didn't even know cows *could* talk. You must be, like, Doctor Doolittle." She whistled "If I Could Talk to the Animals," a song that we learned in elementary school. The ants ate this up like it was their last meal. Philip and Robbie were laughing so hard, I thought they were going to fall out of their seats. I turned my back, disgusted, and trying not to let Lively see that her words were chipping away at me.

Her whistling definitely got to Sandra, though. Her face twitched in about twenty different directions, like she didn't know what expression to make, so she tried to make them all.

"Get *away* from here," she hissed at me through clenched teeth. Her soft words tore into me, doing more damage than any of Lively's harsh ones. "I'll meet you outside the girls' bathroom in H-wing at the end of next period." She pushed past me to dump her tray. As she did, I saw the red barrettes holding back the shorter hairs that wouldn't fit into her ponytail. They matched her shiny ruby earrings.

"How'd it go?" Millie asked when I got back to my seat at the rear of the room. At the next table, the kids went quiet. I glared in their direction. A few blushed and tried to resume conversations.

I turned back to Millie. What could I say?

"Awful." Then I filled her in.

"At least she wants to meet you," she said. "That's something."

I shrugged. "I don't think there's much 'wanting to' at all," I said. "When I showed up, she didn't have a choice. It was the only way she could get rid of me." My anger replaced with sadness, I stuffed my (uneaten) lunch back into my bag, propped my elbows on the table, and sighed. Millie watched me with sympathy.

Mount Celeste had just gone dormant.

Chapter 12

ABOUT TEN MINUTES before the end of science, I asked Mr. Regan for a bathroom pass.

"Can't you wait?" he said. "Class will be over soon. You can go during the passing period." We were doing a lab on Archimedes' principle of buoyancy, so the class was dropping various-sized objects into fish tanks and trying to calculate volume. At least, that was what was supposed to be happening. From what I could tell, most boys in the lab groups were splashing one another or threatening to drop the girls' notebooks into the water. Alan Okuri, one of the smartest boys in school, had finished and was whispering with Mike Arroyo. Alan nudged Mike and they both peeked in our direction. Alan's direct stare made me blush. Millie and I had also finished the experiment and were trying to figure out what I should say to Sandra while watching the boys. So far, we hadn't come up with anything. Alan jostled Mike with an elbow. He slid off his lab stool.

"Well, I kind of can't," I said, turning back to Mr. Regan.

Unable to figure out how to end the sentence, I raised my eyebrows at Millie. *How can I get out of here?* Regan was young, new, and hated to give out bathroom passes.

"Mr. Regan, Celeste has been having cramps since lunch," she said, giving him a "you-know-what-I'm-talking-about" look. Mike, headed in our direction, slunk back to his seat.

Regan made the STOP gesture with his hands. "Fine, Ms. Taposok. That's enough." Then, to me, "Back before the bell and turn in your lab report on your way out." I nodded and offered him a weak smile.

"Did you have to say *that*?" I whispered to Millie when he left.

"Got you out, didn't it?" she said. "Go. Good luck." She shooed me to the front of the room. Moos and whispers of "Skinny Cow" followed as I squeezed between the desks occupied by Lively's friends. A couple of kids watched me with pity.

I took the pass—a plastic thighbone labeled *Femur (always trying to teach us something, isn't he?)*—and moved as fast as my short legs would take me across the building to H-wing. The closer I got, the heavier my heart pounded. The bone was getting slick in my right hand. *What if she's not there? What if she is? What am I going to say to her? Why did I do this?* My empty belly gurgled. I felt like Piggy fumbling around for his glasses on the beach in *Lord of the Flies*.

When I turned the corner into H-wing, I saw Sandra leaning against the wall outside the bathroom door. I hadn't realized how much she'd changed in just two weeks. Her red tank top matched her red and white skirt. Before Lively, Sandra would never wear a tank top to school, let alone a skirt. Soccer shorts and T-shirts were her, well, uniform. The only shoes she owned were either sneakers or cleats. The red strappy sandals on her feet had to belong to her sister, Sarah.

Or Lively, Red Bathing Suit Woman whispered.

I slowed. Sandra pushed the bathroom door open, holding it for me.

I entered without a word. Sandra followed, then leaned against one of the sinks, legs crossed at the ankles and arms folded in front of her chest. I stood across from her, back against the mirror, and tapped my leg with Femur. For what felt like an hour, we stayed like that, watching each other.

"Hey," I began, not sure what I was going to say, mouth as dry as pocket lint. I kept my gaze on the sink to her left. "I just want to know what's going on. What happened?"

"What *happened?*" she said. Her words were as cold as the sundaes we both loved. "What happened was that you were totally embarrassing at lunch. I can't believe you would *do* that to me!"

The Conversation Bus passed my stop. I shook my head and forced my eyes up to meet hers. "What I did to *you?* What are you talking about? You were the one who just *walked away* when—"

"Whatever." Sandra flipped one hand like she was brushing away a fly. "You don't get it, Celeste. Lively is cool. She says mean things sometimes, but she's also really nice and funny when we hang out. I *like* hanging out with her. And so does Robbie Flan."

Someone replaced the bathroom floor with a boat deck, because all of a sudden I couldn't keep my balance. Pain and fear forgotten, I stopped tapping and put my free hand against the cold tile wall to steady myself. "You *do?*"

"I do," she repeated. "That doesn't mean that we can't hang out too. It just means that we'll have to hang out together . . . outside of school." A spot above my head held her attention.

"Outside of school." This time I was the one doing the repeating.

"Yeah." She stood up straight and smoothed her skirt, then gazed into the mirror behind me and patted her hair.

"But we are—were—are best friends," I said. *Lame!* I shouted at myself. It sounded desperate.

"We are," Sandra said, still looking in the mirror. "Best friends—outside of school." Her eyes flicked to mine for a split second, then darted away again.

"Outside of school," I said again. *Now I know how Uncle Chuck feels around Aunt Doreen.*

"Yeah. Look, it's easier that way. I have to get back to social studies before the bell rings. Robbie might want to talk to me. We'll catch up later, okay?"

Easier that way? Throwing your clothes on the floor instead of hanging them up is easier? *Did she really say that?!*

I nodded, but I doubt she saw. The door banged open, and she didn't even give me another glance. I slumped against the wall.

Funny, I didn't know that a "best friend" was supposed to make you feel this miserable. *This is what Theo Christmas means when he sings, "My heart is so dark, you're all I can see in the mirror,"* Red Bathing Suit Woman muttered, her voice bitter.

Thanks for the insight, I retorted.

Chapter 13

THE ONLY GOOD thing about the BBQ Day Incident was that it completely made me forget about Miss Husky-Peach. I trudged through the rest of that day enveloped in a cloud of numbness that covered me like a blanket since the bathroom. I kept hearing Sandra saying, "We can be best friends—outside of school" over and over in my head. Every pound of the Negative Twenty clung to my heart.

I couldn't even explain what happened to Millie. When I got back to science, I just shook my head. Something in my face told her not to ask questions.

The cloud followed me on my walk home, all the way to my front door. Downstairs there was no sign of Mom.

"Celeste, I have something for you to see," she called from the second floor. I went up, listening to Sandra and puffing the whole way.

Mom perched on the foot of my bed, a big bag at her feet and a pile of clothes covering my comforter. Was Theo Christmas smirking from the poster?

"What's all this?" I asked, and slid my backpack to the floor. I wasn't interested, but it seemed like the right thing to say. *"Best friends—outside of school,"* Sandra murmured as an answer.

Mom's smile was as wide as our couch. "I've noticed that you've been making some healthy choices these days. I'm really impressed with how well you've been eating. So, as a treat, I went shopping for you. Plus, you should have something new to wear to the city tomorrow, something fun."

A flood rushed through my body, washing away the Cloud of Numbness and replacing it with a Glacier of Terror. My hands tingled and I shivered. The Miss HuskyPeach interview and photo shoot were the next day.

"Oh," I said, fighting instant panic. "You didn't have to do that. I thought I'd just wear, you know, this." I gestured at my track pants and hoodie.

Mom laughed. "You're too much. Here—go try this on," she said, handing me a purple and black bundle of cloth. "It'll be our own private fashion show."

There was no use arguing. Once the card was mailed in, my fate was sealed. It was easier to pretend like the day would never come, while eating salads and apples just in case it did. And now it had. *At least no one knows,* I thought. *At least I never told Sandra.* It was a small reassurance.

I changed in the bathroom. The outfit consisted of flowy black pants and a purple scoop-necked shirt with wide sleeves. The pants fit okay, but the shirt's sleeves belled out at the wrist and I couldn't figure out what to do with my arms. I settled on holding them out to the side, so they looked like wings.

"That's classy," Mom teased when I came into the room. I raised an eyebrow at her.

"Classy? I don't think that's what we should be going for." From his perch on my wall, Theo agreed.

She stuck her tongue out. "Here's another one," she said, tossing a green shirt at me.

"Too tight," she said when I returned. It transformed my belly into an inner tube. Had Operation Skinny Celeste even touched the Negative Twenty?

HuskyPeach, here I come, I thought.

And that's how it went: I tried stuff on, she commented. We finally settled on the black pants and an orange wrap-style top with a black tank thing underneath. Well, Mom settled. Even though I told her I felt like a pumpkin, she insisted it looked the best on me. I was too tired to argue. Even Theo was worn out, drooping over his guitar and wearing a tired smile.

I spent the rest of the evening in a mental tug-of-war: worry a little about Sandra, a little about the HuskyPeach. Exhausted and stressed out, I barely picked at dinner after not eating any lunch.

Well, I thought, *at least I don't have to worry about writing anything in the food log tonight.*

The next morning, Saturday, I took so long getting ready that Mom ended up sitting in the car and honking the horn to get me out of the house. Dad and Ben stood at the foot of the stairs, cheering and hooting as I came out of my room.

"There's our beauty queen!" Dad called.

"Whooo!" shouted Ben, clapping. He jumped and gave me a high five as I passed by, then banged his elbow on the banister.

After we got the ice pack, they cheered the whole way to the car. In spite of my nerves, I smiled.

"Just be yourself," Dad yelled as we pulled away. "They'll love you!"

That's what I'm afraid of, I thought. But it gave me an idea.

There was a big sign welcoming the First Annual Northern California Regional PeachWear Modeling Challenge Contestants hung above the company's main door.

Please don't let anyone I know see me going in, I thought.

"Here we go," Mom said, parking the car in the lot across the street. My stomach dropped to my knees. When she said, "Just do your best, sweetheart. That's all we expect," I felt even worse.

Inside, skinny women wearing tiny black dresses and gold name tags shuttled us up to the fourth-floor office suite where the interview and photo shoot would take place. There were about a dozen other moms and girls crammed into a conference room. A table, pushed against the far wall, held two platters of cookies and brownies, plus bowls of chips and salsa. Most of the moms were busy primping their daughters: spritzing, patting, blotting, straightening, smoothing, and buzzing last-minute instructions in their ears.

The girls eyed one another like cats do before they fight, and chewed their snacks. Some were larger than me, but all of us had the same basic shape: round, round, round. A surprise: They were pretty. All of them. Not drop-dead gorgeous, mind you, but they all had nice features, in spite of their roundness. Come to think of it, I hadn't seen this many pretty girls together in one place in my life. Why was I here? One girl wore the purple shirt I tried on the day before. She didn't know what to do with the sleeves either. I smiled at her, but her mother scooted her away.

I wonder how many of them have best friends "outside of school"?

Mom and I stepped away from the door as it opened. A thin red-haired woman came in alone. She wore a charcoal-colored business suit and the largest diamond ring that I'd ever seen. Its sparkle would blind Lively and her groupies for sure. *Or show Sandra how fake those girls are,* I thought.

"Welcome to PeachWear, and thank you for coming," she said. The buzz stopped. "I'm Patricia Markowitz, vice president of marketing for PeachWear. We're so glad you joined us today." A murmur slid around the room.

"You are a very special group. Our judges hand-selected you to be here because they feel that you have the qualities that PeachWear represents. Out of two hundred and fifty applicants, you twelve were selected to represent us." She paused to let the number sink in. In spite of what I was there for, I was impressed. I'd never been picked for anything, and they'd received a lot of applications. Mom must've thought so too, because she squeezed my shoulder and gave me a smile.

"This is our first year conducting the challenge, and we wanted to make sure the contestants were the very best of the bunch. We're looking for girls who are bright, bubbly, and enthusiastic about living life to the fullest." She smiled at the crowd. "Our models have an appetite for life, and—"

She did not just say that!

"—our goal is to show that to the world.

"Now, please let me introduce the Modeling Challenge Coordinators. You'll be working closely with them over the next couple of weeks. Erika Snee, PeachWear's Northern California Marketing Director—"

The door opened and one of the skinny women in black entered to courtesy claps.

"I'm sure you are all familiar with our celebrity coordinator and former HuskyPeach model," Patricia continued, "Violet Page." The polite claps grew into real applause, and a couple of the girls whistled and jumped up and down. The floor shook.

"Who is she?" Mom whispered in my ear.

"Dunno. *Where* is she?" I whispered back. The door remained closed. The applause and cheers died down. Patricia did not look happy. She whispered something to Erika, who seemed less happy that Patricia, and who then left the room. Patricia offered us a brittle smile. "I'm sure she'll be with us in a moment."

A few seconds later, the door did open. The applause

started again, accompanied by squeals and hoots. Erika slipped back into the room, followed by a woman who had to be Violet Page. She was super tall, had long honey-colored hair, wide gray eyes framed by long lashes, and perfect skin. Violet Page was not skinny. Although not as round as some of the contestants, she was definitely what you'd call "husky." And she was beautiful.

Mom, never concerned about embarrassing herself, tugged on the sleeve of the woman standing next to her who was applauding with enthusiasm. "Excuse me," Mom said in response to the woman's dirty look, "can you tell me who Violet Page is?"

The woman blinked and stopped clapping. "Are you kidding?" When Mom shook her head, she continued. "Only the most famous plus-sized model in the world. And she's going to be launching my—I mean, *our*—daughters' careers."

Chapter 14

THAT'S *WHO PAUL was talking about at dinner!*

Before I could get any further into my thoughts, Erika broke the twelve contestants into groups of four for our interviews and photo shoots. She said over and over again that they wanted us to be "bubbly and engaging" during our conversations. One group would interview first, while the other two would start with the photos. *Kind of like gym class,* I thought. That was quickly followed by a memory of Yurk Fest, which I pushed away. *No need to replace anyone else's shoes.* (Coach Anapoli's gift card was still wedged in the bottom of my backpack.) But I would make things difficult, and if the plan I thought of on the ride up worked, there'd be no need for me to come back for round two—no matter what Mom said.

I was in the first-round interview group, along with the daughter of the woman who told us who Violet Page was, the girl in the purple bell-sleeved shirt, and a chunky Asian girl. One of the women in black led our moms and us down a hall to another conference room. "You'll wait in here, and each contestant will be interviewed in the next room," she said, standing outside the conference room.

"Alone?" Violet Page Explainer Mom asked.

The guide nodded. This was not the response VPE Mom wanted. She argued with our escort, explaining she needed to support her bay-be. *Sounds like Aunt Doreen,* I thought. Her curly-haired daughter stood to the side, studying the carpet. The rest of us filed past them into the room. Our guide closed the door, remaining in the hall to deal with VPE Mom.

Mom nudged me. "Isn't this exciting," she said, turning her head to take in the scene. I shrugged.

We sat at a small table (also holding snacks)—*how much do they want us to eat?*—and waited. Across from us sat the purple-shirt daughter and her mother; the other contestant sat at the far end of the table. The ones across from us had the same pear shape, light brown hair, and button noses. They were also wearing enough makeup to cover the faces on Mount Rushmore.

"Just remember what we talked about, honey. Answer everything with a smile and don't forget to tell them about your volunteer work at the hospital and the time you had your picture in the newspaper."

"I won't," the girl said, a tinge of irritation in her voice. She shifted in her seat every few seconds, trying not to wrinkle the sleeves on her awkward shirt. When her mom turned away, she rolled her eyes at me and smirked over her mother's behavior. I smiled.

"Hey," she said.

"Hi," I responded.

"Ashley, listen to me," her mother cut us off. "This is very important. This is your future we're talking about. How are you going to win with that attitude?" And on and on and on, while Ashley fumed.

So glad my mom didn't try to coach me, I thought. I turned to give her a grateful smile, and caught the alarmed expression on her face. *Guess she doesn't feel that way.*

"Do you know what you're going to say?" she said in a low voice, so as not to disturb Ashley's mother. (Truthfully, an explosion probably wouldn't have disturbed that woman. She was still telling Ashley not to forget the dog show, Honors Algebra, and Girl Scouts.)

I nodded. "I'm good. Don't worry."

Mom shook her head. "I won't. Just remember how proud of you we are." She raised her head to glance around the room. "Maybe we should introduce ourselves," she said, putting a cheerful tone in her voice. "Seeing that we're going to be in this together today." The other mothers shifted in their seats.

They take this pretty seriously, Red Bathing Suit Woman whispered to me. *They should relax.*

After a few more seconds of uncomfortable silence, the Asian girl—who had long, enviable hair that flowed to her butt—spoke.

"I'm Gail Wu," she started, her voice low and unsure. "I'm a freshman at Pally High, and—"

"Don't forget to tell them what year you are in school,"

Ashley's mother interrupted to remind her daughter. Gail slumped in her seat. Gail's mother, a birdlike woman who made Aunt Doreen look like a HuskyPeach, glared at the other mom.

"Mom!" Ashley of the Awkward-Sleeved Shirt chided. "That is so rude! I'm sorry," she directed to Gail, who straightened up again. She introduced herself, then went on, "I'm a sophomore at East. You're . . ." She turned to me.

"Celeste," I said, shy around these older girls. "Eighth grade at AlHo." If Gail and Ashley were surprised to be in a group with someone younger than them, they didn't show it.

The door opened, and VPE Mom and her daughter, the blond girl who stared at the floor and seemed about sixteen, came into the room, followed by our now frazzled-looking guide.

"Ashley Freeman," she said, like the nurse at the doctor's office. "The interview team is ready for you now."

As Ashley slid back from the table, her mother's chatter became even faster. "Don't-forget-about-honors-block-and-color-guard-and-how-much-you-love-animals-and—" The click of the closing door cut her off. She slumped in her chair and turned to my mom.

"I just want her to do well," she said, like it was an apology. Mom nodded.

"I know."

"I mean, it's just a regional competition, but it could lead to bigger things." My mom nodded again. At the end of the table, Mrs. Wu fiddled with Gail's hair clip.

VPE Mom took her daughter to the corner of the room, where they huddled. Based on their body language, they were planning a high-risk, dangerous mission. The rest of us sat in near silence for the ten minutes Ashley was out. At one point, her mom eyed the brownies.

"Have one," my mom said, sliding the tray in her direction.

"Oh, I couldn't," she replied, patting her belly. "Got to watch those calories."

Somehow, I think I was the only one who found that funny.

Everyone jumped when Ashley returned. Gail let out a surprised squeak. Ashley's mother sprang from her chair and crossed the room. "How was it?" she asked, gripping her daughter's upper arms. Ashley shrugged, but I didn't get to hear her response.

"Celeste Harris," the escort said.

My stomach dropped in a scary reminder of Yurk Fest. I was glad I hadn't eaten any of the snacks.

"The team is ready for you now."

Mom squeezed my hand. I was glad she did. Time to put my plan into action.

Bubbly and engaging, I coached myself. *Just* don't *be "bubbly and engaging."*

Chapter 15

THE "TEAM" CONSISTED of Erika and Violet, and the conference room they were parked in was a mirror of the one next door. Only instead of snacks on the table, Erika and Violet had piles of paper in front of them. Well, Erika had a pile of paper in front of her. Violet was filing her nails.

"Ms. Harris, have a seat," Erika said, after offering me her hand to shake. It was cold and bony. Violet only smiled. Up close, I could see that she was young—maybe twenty. She was prettier than Lively by far—and just as pretty as Kirsten and Kathleen, even though she was big. Violet returned to her filing.

I sat.

"Why don't you tell us a little bit about yourself," Erika said, reading from a sheet. She shuffled her papers and waited for me to begin.

This is it; no going back now. I took a deep breath.

"I'm thirteen and in eighth grade." I bit my tongue to keep from saying more.

They waited. After a few seconds, Erika raised an eyebrow. Violet paid no attention.

"Is there anything else you'd like to add, Ms. Harris?" Erika asked.

"No, thank you. That's all." *No reason to be impolite.*

Erika shifted in her seat. "Let's try another one. I think you need to get warmed up," she said. She scanned her list for another question. "Tell us about school. What subjects do you like?"

"Language Arts," I replied. "I read a lot."

"What do you like to read?" Erika asked.

"Well," I said, trying to decide how to be nice but not *too* nice, "we just finished reading *The Lord of the Flies.* I kind of liked the gory parts."

It seemed that Erika didn't have a prepared response to that answer. She shuffled her papers. After a moment, she tried again. "Do you participate in any activities?"

"Not really. I don't play any sports," I said, "and the last time we ran in gym class I yurked on my teacher's shoes." *Where did* that *come from?* I thought. I hadn't meant to bring that up.

"Yurked?" Erika asked, her face scrunching into the question.

"Um, I think it's like 'barf,' right, Celeste?" Violet said, the corners of her mouth twitching to avoid a smile. I nodded, my face hot. Erika looked as though she'd just bitten into a lemon.

"Whom do you most admire?" she said, probably trying to find a "safe" question on her list.

I considered my options—my mom, presidents, world leaders. *That's what a good HuskyPeach would say.*

"Theo Christmas," I responded, satisfied with my unusual choice. Violet dropped her nail file. I glanced at her. Was she blushing?

"That singer? Who plays guitar?" Erika squeaked.

I gave a strong nod.

"Why him?" Violet asked, leaning over the table.

"Why not?" I responded, an unintentional edge in my voice.

"Urm. Okay, then. What made you want to be a HuskyPeach model?" Erika read, moving on. She gave me a wide, fake smile.

"I don't really know how to answer that," I said, telling the truth. They waited.

Violet, whose color was back to normal—had I imagined that blush?—sat straighter. "Maybe we should be asking Celeste *who* made her want to be a HuskyPeach model." She raised an eyebrow.

"That's ridiculous," Erika snapped at Violet. "You can't talk to contestants that way. She's just nervous. Right, Celeste? It's okay," she said, maybe trying to convince herself.

"Actually, my aunt entered me in the contest," I said, telling more truths. Well, kind of. Violet's smile widened. Erika ignored my answer.

"We'll ask another question."

Erika read from her paper: "The HuskyPeach wants girls to express their true identity and embrace life. Can you give an example of how you show your true self to the world?" She smiled. "Who are you, Celeste? Who are you, really?"

Are they kidding? Like I have any idea. Especially this week.

Honesty is definitely the best policy in those situations.

"I have no idea," I said.

Violet laughed so hard, milk would have come out her nose if she were drinking some. Erika grimaced and gritted her teeth.

"That's great," Violet said, chuckling. Erika's glare would've wilted plants.

"I'm not sure that's the response we're looking for," she protested. She did a good job of keeping her voice even, but the crumpled paper in her hands and the vein throbbing in her temple gave away her real feelings.

"Oh, whatever, Erika. She's being honest. I bet she's the only one we see today who doesn't rattle off some fake prepared answers to these questions." Violet rolled her eyes and moved her arm as though waving off the other contestants.

I sat there and struggled with my Mask of Innocence—trying not to laugh with Violet. Later, when I had time to think about the day, I'd probably feel bad about some of my answers, but right then I was enjoying myself. *Take that, Aunt Doreen,* I thought. And, even though she had nothing to do with the situation, *Take that, Lively. And Sandra* (for good measure).

"Oh look, our time's up," Erika said, relief visible on her face. The vein even stopped pulsing. "Thank you for coming in. You may go back to the conference room and wait for the next segment of the Challenge." She recited her memorized speech quickly.

"How'd it go?" Mom asked when I closed the door behind me. Bay-be, the curly-haired blond girl, slipped out for her interview. Her mother started pacing.

"Depends on who you ask," I said. Then I finally laughed.

Chapter 16

ONCE EVERYONE HAD been interviewed, Frazzled Guide led us down to the photo shoot, which was on the third floor. VPE Mom trailed two steps behind her the whole way, asking questions to make sure that she wouldn't be separated from her bay-be for the rest of the contest. Her daughter followed, eyes glued to the ground.

Ashley and Gail fell into step beside me.

"How'd it go," Ashley spoke under her breath. Her mother was in front of us.

"I didn't say much," I replied, still telling the truth. "It wasn't my idea to do this."

Ashley nodded. "I know what you mean. Seemed like a good idea at the time, but now . . ." She trailed off. Her mother, suddenly aware that Ashley wasn't by her side, encouraged her to keep up.

Gail shook her head. "My mom is just as terrified as I am," she said, watching Ashley's mother pilot Ashley down the hall and away from us. "But I'm glad she's not like *that*."

She said the last part in a whisper. I bit the inside of my cheek to keep from laughing out loud.

We entered a large room with a gray sheet (we were told it's called a backdrop) hanging in front of one wall. Giant lights stood on spider legs in a semicircle in front of it. A plain box about chair height was planted in between the lights and the sheet.

That was the only empty spot in the whole space. Behind the lights, people scurried in all directions: barking orders, calling names, moving parents, and arranging contestants. Girls perched in folding canvas chairs were being primped, smoothed, spritzed, and blotted by skinny people wearing white smocks to cover their black clothes (too much primping, smoothing, spritzing, and blotting was going on, in my opinion). And, of course, the table of snacks stood in the corner. *Do they move them from room to room?* My belly rumbled. *Do snacks at the modeling challenge count against Operation Skinny Celeste?* I edged toward the brownies.

Do you really want to find out if they do? Red Bathing Suit Woman answered. I ignored her, heading for the tray.

Frazzled Guide addressed our group, foiling my Subtle Brownie Maneuver. "Each contestant will be assigned a stylist to do a final prep for the shoot. When your name is called, you will move to the set for your photo series. The photographer will give you specific instructions regarding poses at that time." She kept an eye on VPE Mom. "Do you have any questions?"

VPE Mom didn't disappoint. "Will we be able to make suggestions to the stylist? My bay-be has very difficult hair."

Our group turned to Bay-be. Seemed curly, blond, and uncomplicated to me. The girl flushed scarlet and stared at the floor.

"The stylists are just here to freshen the girls," Frazzled Guide responded, through clenched teeth. "They will not change their existing hair or makeup unless absolutely necessary. Each stylist spends only ten minutes with his or her contestant. You may," she added, "give the stylist suggestions if you wish." She gave VPE Mom a tight smile.

A few minutes later, I met my stylist. Christian was short, had bleached blond hair, and held a round brush like a magic wand in one hand and a giant espresso in the other. He pecked my mom on the cheek and stepped back to take me in.

"Love the wrap shirt," he said. Mom beamed. "Great choice. It defines your waist and the color wakes you right up." As he spoke, he hustled me to a canvas chair. "Let's see. No makeup on you today. Do you ever wear makeup?" He barely waited for me to shake my head. "I can tell." He winked.

As much as I didn't want to like someone called a "stylist," I liked Christian. He wasn't reading from a script. Unlike Erika, he made me feel comfortable, and he darted around his station like a honey bee in a flower shop—only twice as fast and with triple the caffeine.

"Okay," he said, addressing both me and my mom, "you have great skin. I'm not going to spackle you or make you look like someone you're not, so don't worry."

I hadn't realized I was holding my breath until he said that. I exhaled.

"So what are you going to do?" Mom asked.

He rummaged in a big box next to me, sorting through tubes, bottles, compacts, and pots until he found what he was looking for: a big pouffy makeup brush.

"Enhance," he said with another wink. "That's all she needs."

With that, I opened, closed, pursed, raised, kissed, and turned whenever he told me to. Then he juggled his Round Brush of Magic, a blow dryer, and a bottle of hairspray. What seemed like a blast and a squirt later, he announced, "You're done."

He stepped aside, and Mom got a good look at me. Her hands flew to her face. "Oh!" was all she said.

Just like that day in Angelique's, I thought. Fear seeped through me. I don't know what expression was on my face, but it couldn't have been good. Christian rushed to my side.

"Trust me, you look great," he said in my ear, and handed me a mirror. "She's a little surprised, that's all."

I was afraid to look. Christian gave me an encouraging nod. I took a deep breath, and then raised the mirror.

That's me? I almost didn't recognize myself. My hair surrounded my face in a soft wave. My eyes were as large as those spotlights they use for movie premiers, but framed by long lashes and lightly shadowed lids. Somehow, Christian even got them to sparkle like Mom's. Instead of their normal shade of Embarrassed Red, my cheeks were rosy, pale pink. Same with my lips. The whole effect was incredible. Celeste the Cow, Spew, Fat Girl—all of those people were gone. A new Celeste—Celeste the Model—was in the chair. *This* girl wouldn't throw up on her gym teacher's shoes. Or let Lively Carson steal her best friend. I could get to like this girl.

"Honey," Mom gasped, finally able to speak, "you look beautiful."

"You like it?" Christian asked. "I was worried for a second."

"I can't believe it," she said. Now I understood why people like Lively stared at their own reflections all the time. There was no way I was going to put that mirror down. *Maybe Mom would let Christian move in with us.*

"You can do this at home," he said. "It's easy. Here, I'll show you." He reached into his Box of Beauty and Enchantment, but must have cast the wrong spell, because Frazzled Guide appeared.

"Celeste, you're great," she said, eyes on her watch. "It's time for your shoot."

"But I—but he was just—" I tried. *Please don't make me leave the chair.*

"But they were—" Mom began. She looked as disappointed as I felt.

"We're on a tight schedule," she said. "Let's go."

Christian gave me a grin. "I'll show you next time. You're assigned to me for the next two sessions." As he was speaking, he scooted me out of the chair and over to the backdrop, where Bay-be was finishing her turn. She shot dazzling smiles and coy glances at the camera like a pro.

"Has she done this before?" I murmured.

A peck on the cheek and a "smile pretty!" later, I was

sitting on the box facing a very large camera, lots of lights, and a dark shadow that was supposed to be a photographer named Nate. Christian made my mom disappear too. The giant lights blinded me, and I squinted into them trying to find her.

"Hold!" came from a figure behind the brightness. "Celeste, you can't squint. Open your eyes, put your shoulders back, and turn to the camera." It was close to the summer thunder sound of my dad's voice when he's upset, so I obeyed. Fast.

I guess Shadow Nate took a picture, because the next thing he said was, "Great. Tilt your head a little to the right. No, the other right. That's it. Hold."

What kind of pictures were these? I definitely wasn't smiling for them. *Not that I was planning to anyway*, I reminded myself. *But if they don't want me to . . .*

I flashed what Ben would call a "cheese-eating" grin at the camera. With my head tilted, I was sure it would come out goofy, not like Bay-be's movie star dazzler.

The Shadow tossed directions at me one after the other— tilt this way, then that, lift this shoulder, lower that one—stuff that I couldn't imagine turning out well in a picture. Each time he asked for a smile, I gave a big toothy one. When he said, "Serious now," I tried my hardest to look super serious, furrowing my eyebrows and kind of frowning. There was no way those photos could be good, which was a shame considering Christian's efforts to transform me.

If The Shadow was frustrated, though, he didn't show it. After every shot he said the same thing: "Great."

If my hair was on fire and llamas came to put it out, he'd tell me the shot was great, I thought.

When I'd twisted, turned, and lifted enough, Shadow Nate told me I was finished. *Round one is done,* I thought. *Obligation over.* I slid off the box and walked into the light. Then straight through, into the darkness.

The spots were so bright, I couldn't see anything after I passed them. Dots danced across my vision and starbursts replaced people. I should have stopped walking when I realized that I was blind, but I didn't. I just wanted to find Mom and go home. So I took three more steps—right into someone small and bony. Who I knocked to the floor.

Then tripped over.

And fell on.

Contestants, moms, and stylists came running from all directions. I heard an angry "Get *off* me!" from somewhere around my middle. A sharp elbow or knee jabbed my belly. My vision hadn't cleared, so I couldn't tell which way to go, but I needed to pick a direction, quick. I rolled to my right.

"OW!"

Wrong way. Being round makes it hard to spring to my feet. Hands grasped my shoulders and heaved. I came to my knees and blinked hard. Below me, I could see Erika's scowling face through a spotlight starburst.

Don't have to try to throw the contest anymore, I thought. Based on her expression, I had about the same chance of winning as Ben had of growing up without getting another bump or bruise.

Chapter 17

MOM SPENT THE entire ride home from San Francisco chattering about how *great* the day was, and how *beautiful* I looked, and how *wonderful* the experience was. When I pointed out that Erika did not have a *wonderful* experience or a *great* day, she scowled and chided me for Focusing on the Negative. "Models have to look on the bright side of things," she said. "Keeps them from breaking out. Besides, you looked so good, I think you need to go back for round two."

"But we agreed!" I protested. I'd met my obligation. What more did she want from me?

"Honey, you aren't seriously considering quitting now," she said, surprise in her voice. "Didn't you see yourself? You were like a different person in there."

Yeah . . . Miss HuskyPeach-person, Red Bathing Suit Woman snickered. I did my best to ignore her, but she was right.

"Why do I have to be different?" I barked. "Why can't I just be *me?*"

"Sweetie, you're wonderful just as you are." Mom's eyes slid from the road for a quick glance at me. She gave me a warm smile. "But like Christian said, this was you—enhanced. Confident, beautiful . . . radiant. You were a star. Don't you think that's what you deserve? I do."

"I said I'd only go once," I muttered.

"But didn't you like Christian? And those girls in our group seemed nice. Plus, you could learn a lot from watching Violet Page in the next round." Her tone switched to neutral, but her hands gripped the steering wheel hard.

She can't be serious, I thought. She sounded like the other pageant moms. I made a mental note not to let her talk to Ashley's mother ever again, then kept my mouth shut and fumed during the rest of the ride. No matter what I said, I knew I'd be sucked into going back for round two. My non-interview and steamrolling of Erika had to be enough to make me lose the contest, but Christian's magic brush worked some serious charm. Operation Skinny Celeste would have to continue for another two weeks. The Negative Twenty *had* to come off.

By the time we pulled into our driveway, thanks to Mom's endless conversation and my anxiety party, I was wound as tightly as a jack-in-the-box. I popped out of the car and scooted inside, hoping to go straight to my room, change, and return to my old life (well, maybe after I got another look in the mirror at Model Celeste).

Ben was sitting on the stairs, threading laces into a pair of sneakers. "You look different," he said as I stepped over him. "What'd they do to you there?"

"Hair and makeup," I muttered, heaving myself up the steps, puffing. *Certainly don't feel any different.*

"Some girls are waiting for you," he called after me.

I froze. *Some girls? Who? Couldn't be Sandra, could it? Who would be with her?* The answer came instantly. *Lively.* Sandra and Lively were waiting for me. Maybe they were sorry. Maybe Sandra felt bad about what happened in the bathroom, and was bringing Lively to apologize about the cafeteria.

What do I say?

"Hell-ooo, spacey," Ben sang. "Are you going up there or what?"

I turned to the sound of his voice. "Who's waiting?" I forced out through my dry mouth.

He shrugged and finished lacing. "Dunno. Some girls. I can't remember their names."

Ben's known Sandra since he was three. He'd tell me if she were in my room. Relieved that it wasn't Sandra, I continued up the steps. *Has to be Katy and Millie,* I thought. *But why would they be here? They don't know about the HuskyPeach.* Then I froze again. They *didn't* know about the HuskyPeach. What was I going to tell them—"Oh, I just get dressed up like this on the weekends"? I groaned.

My bedroom door was closed, but laughter seeped from its cracks. I tried to swipe my hair back in its usual messy knot, but Christian made my hair clip disappear too. Giving up, I grabbed the knob with a slick hand and twisted.

Katy and Millie were perched on my bed, each holding one of my yellow and green plaid throw pillows in their laps and wearing matching startled expressions. Even Theo

Christmas seemed surprised. It felt like I interrupted a private conversation, which was weird since the private conversation was going on in my room.

"Hey," Katy started, "hope it's okay." She gestured with the pillow to encompass the whole room. "Your dad said we could hang out until you got home."

"Yeah," Millie added. She tugged on a pink earring. "We wanted to hear about what happened with Sandra, 'cause you seemed really upset yesterday, so we came over."

"And your brother told us where you were, so we decided to stay until you got back," Katy finished. "Celeste, you look *amazing*." Her eyes were wide.

My face warmed. *I could murder Ben*, I thought. *Should've told him not to tell anyone about this.* But until now, it hadn't occurred to me that I *had* anyone to tell. Millie and Katy were worried about me, and came over to see how I was doing—which was more than Sandra had done in weeks.

They made room on the bed. Millie patted a patch of green comforter. I sat, legs dangling over the edge, and picked at the fringe on one of the pillows.

"It happened really fast," I started, "and I really didn't want it to, and with everything else going on, I just never said anything."

"It's exciting," Millie said. "You're a model."

I shook my head. "Not exactly." I sighed. "It's kind of a long story . . ."

"All your brother said was that you were in the city for a modeling shoot," Katy explained. "So fill us in." She settled back against the headboard.

Millie said, "Is this the contest they're advertising at the HuskyPeach store in the mall?" A weight settled in my stomach. I nodded.

"I've seen some signs for it," she said.

"You shop there?" I asked, so surprised that my anxiety lifted.

Millie laughed. "Of course! Where else am I going to find pants to fit my stubby legs? Mom gets them shortened."

"Oh." It never occurred to me that Millie might be a HuskyPeach too. Her admission made it easier for me to start.

"First, you have to swear not to tell anyone else." They promised, then I told them everything, beginning with Aunt Doreen and Mom seeing the flyer at Angelique's, to Operation Skinny Celeste and nearly squashing Erika. They asked one or two questions, but just listened for the most part. When I told them who the celebrity judge was, Millie squealed.

"No way! Did you get to talk to Violet Page?"

I admitted that I had, but hadn't known who she was before starting the contest.

"You're missing out, Celeste. She's amazing," Millie said, squeezing my hand and bouncing on the bed with excitement. "She does all these cool photo shoots, gets invited to celebrity parties, and has some mystery boyfriend."

"Really?" I responded, then went on with my story. The more I spoke, the lighter I felt inside. Once or twice I even laughed. At the time, I hadn't thought any of it was funny. Now that it was over, I felt different. *Maybe different enough to go back?* Red Bathing Suit Woman asked. I pushed the question away.

"And then we came home, and you were here," I finished. While talking, I braided the fringe along one edge of the pillow. I held my hands up, palms to the ceiling, and shrugged. "That's it."

"Whoa," Millie said. "That's crazy. So you have to go back again?"

I nodded. "Mom wants me to. I can't say no. She'll be disappointed."

Katy wore her Thinking Face: eyes narrowed, forehead scrunched. "And you've been dieting this whole time?"

My face heated up again. "Well, only since I found out I was a contestant," I said. "Just a couple of weeks. I've been writing everything down since we got the nutrition information in gym class. I took extra food logs."

"How much weight have you lost?" she asked.

I shifted on the bed, uncomfortable. "A couple of pounds, maybe," I said, lying. I had no idea. "I haven't actually weighed myself." Truth. I'd been avoiding the scale. I was afraid that not an ounce of the Negative Twenty had come off. "But I've been eating lots of fruit and vegetables, and not as many cookies." *And I really miss them,* I added in my head.

Katy nodded, still concentrating. "Scientifically, the only way to lose weight is to burn more energy than you consume. All food is energy. Eating less—or better stuff—helps, but you need to burn more energy. *If* you still want to lose the contest," she said, looking at me. "But you look really good."

I smiled. "Trust me, I still want to lose. Just think of what Lively and everyone would say if I were Miss HuskyPeach." They nodded.

"We can help you, if you want," Katy said after a moment.

"You can?" I asked.

"We can?" Millie repeated, as curious as me.

"Sure. Keep eating what you're eating, and just do more stuff: Go outside, exercise. We can go with you." Katy shrugged. "It's easy."

"For you, maybe," I said, remembering how I lost my breath just going up stairs.

"It'll be fun," Millie said. "Besides, with Christian's help, you'll be the best-looking non-model the HuskyPeach has ever seen."

I smiled again. With all the grinning I'd been doing, my face might freeze that way. *Not that that would be a bad thing,* I thought, looking at Katy and Millie. "Sounds good to me."

I wasn't able to put Millie and Katy's plan into effect right away. Operation Skinny Celeste was replaced by Operation Sniffly Celeste, because for the next two days I was stuck inside with a cold. I sniffled my way around the house and to and from school, so the only energy I burned was from blowing my nose. On the bright side, the only food I wanted was soup. If Oreos leaped from the package and danced into my room, I wouldn't have cared.

By Tuesday I felt better. A good thing too, because Mom and I needed to meet Kirsten and Aunt Doreen at Angelique's for another dress fitting. I packed my pockets with tissues and returned to where my Husky Nightmare began. Aunt Doreen and Kirsten were already waiting for us in the store.

"We had Angelique bring both dresses up so the girls could try them on," Aunt Doreen called as we entered. "She's getting them now." She leaned over to give me a kiss and I sneezed.

"I'm sick, Auntie." I snuffled.

"I can see that," she said, backing away. She turned to my mom and they chatted about centerpieces.

"Hey," Kirsten said, leading me a few steps away. "Heard that the first round of the contest went really well. Did you change your mind or something?"

I hadn't spoken with Kirsten since my explosion in the kitchen two weeks earlier. My cheeks reddened to match my overblown nose. "No, but, um, I'm not going to win. I'm just, uh, trying to get it over with."

Kirsten tried to hide her disappointment, but she didn't do that good a job. Her face said "dishrag" all over it.

"Oh. Well, that's cool, if that's what you want," she said with a small shrug.

My chest tightened. I wanted to explain my decision to her—to say that it just wasn't that easy for me to tell my mom no, or about Operation Skinny Celeste, or that I kind of liked the person Christian turned me into—but trying to do that in the middle of Angelique's when my mom and Aunt Doreen were nearby was too complicated.

Luckily, I didn't have to say anything else. Kirsten changed the subject. "Listen, Celeste, can you remind Sandra and her friends to stop visiting her brother at work? Geoff's going to get in trouble if his boss catches him with those girls one more time. They're always at the McGees' too. "

Before I could tell her that *she* had a better chance of running into Sandra, Angelique appeared, two dresses in her arms and pins in her mouth, nodding in the direction of the dressing room. She gave me a puzzled look as I went by, glancing down at my pants and back to my face.

"Be careful of ze pins on ze bottom," Angelique barked through the slatted door as I was changing. "Yours isn't done yet."

Not wanting to stab myself, I was extra-careful. As I was wriggling into the Monstrosity, I heard Mom and Aunt Doreen carry their conversation into the fitting room area. Kirsten's door opened.

"It looks gorge-*ous*," Aunt Doreen squealed. "It's per-*fect*."

It's déjà vu, I thought. Only this time, my dress fit better. I wasn't sure if Angelique knew Christian, but there was magic going on in this bridal shop. The dress didn't give me the tight, bunchy feeling that it had at our last visit, and it was approaching the right length. Even the sleeves were more comfortable. Before Aunt Doreen or Mom could start nagging me, I slipped out of the dressing room.

Kirsten stood on the carpeted platform, blond hair sweeping across the back of the dress, golden skin glowing through the lace overlay. Reflected over and over in the triple mirror, she was perfect in it. I imagined how beautiful she'd be with her hair done, holding her flowers . . . and then pictured myself, a peach blob on the altar next to her. I blinked the image away.

"Zis one is ready to go," said Angelique, crouched and examining Kirsten's hemline with a critical eye. "Everything is fine." Kirsten stepped off the platform and gave me a wave before ducking into her dressing room.

Mom and Aunt Doreen turned.

"Honey," Mom gushed, "it looks much, much better." Her smile lit up the room. I hiked the trailing fabric and climbed up.

It did. Where it had been stretched and wrinkled, it was now smooth. For the first time, I saw how it would look when Angelique completed the alterations. And although I'd never wear it as well as Kirsten, its Monstrous Awfulness would be because of the dress, not me.

Some of Christian's makeup magic wouldn't hurt the results either, I thought. Maybe I'd be a peach . . . well, *peach*, on the altar, instead of a blob.

"You are a miracle worker, Angelique," Aunt Doreen said. She swiped a hand over my butt to smooth a stray wrinkle. I furrowed my eyebrows and scooted away from her hand.

"I don't think it's all Angelique," Mom said, a smile playing at the corners of her lips. "There have been a lot more healthy choices made in our house lately."

I watched my face darken in the mirror. *Guess Mom's been paying more attention to the apple vs. chocolate cookie consumption than I thought.* Aunt Doreen opened her mouth to speak.

"It will be ready on the sixteenth," Angelique said, heading off embarrassing questions and buzzing around my feet with her pins and tape measure. "The wedding is the nineteenth, no? Plenty of time. Turn," she directed.

When I did, the color drained from Mom's face. Her hands flew to the sides of her head in a way that would have been funny if her expression weren't so horrified. "Oh no," she murmured.

"Noelle, what's the matter?" Aunt Doreen used her panicky voice. "Are you okay? Do you need a doctor?"

Mom shook her head. "N—no, I'm fine. I just . . . forgot that the wedding was on the nineteenth for a second there. I, um, was thinking about something else." Her face regained its color, then passed normal pink and moved right to the popular shade of Embarrassed Celeste Red.

What's with her? I thought. *What could possibly—*

Then I knew.

The final event for the Modeling Challenge is on May 19! That's what bothered me the night that I examined the brochure. I knew there was something important about that date. I couldn't believe that I'd forgotten! For a second, I felt bad for my mom. Disappointment radiated from her. I mean, there'd be no way that I could do both, and Kathleen's wedding was much more important. But then I realized, *I don't have to worry about it anymore! No more Operation Skinny Celeste, no more interviews, no more Frazzled Guide, no more annoying moms. It's over!*

I wanted to jump down and do a Dance of Freedom and Joy right in front of Aunt Doreen, Mom, and Angelique— and Kirsten, when she finished changing. But I stayed put. Best to play it cool.

"What were you thinking about?" Aunt Doreen asked, eyes narrowed. "Because whatever it was gave you a bad spell."

"Nothing, nothing," Mom said. "I just thought there was a conflict with something else. That's all."

"But you've known about the wedding for *months*," Aunt Doreen said, voice rising. "What could conflict?"

The tension between my mom and aunt was as thick as oatmeal.

Kirsten, I noticed, hadn't come out of her dressing room. Smart. Meanwhile, Angelique did her best to stay invisible by hiding behind me.

"Well, um," Mom began, glancing to me for help. Which she didn't get. "I thought there might be a conflict with the HuskyPeach Modeling Challenge, but there isn't," she said, rushing her words.

"What do you *mean*?" Aunt Doreen's voice was ear-piercing. "Noelle, you tell me *right now* if Celeste isn't going to be at my daughter's wedding." Now *her* face turned red, although it was Crimson Fury as opposed to Celeste Red.

"Well, you entered her," my mother snapped, face hard, "so don't be upset that *I* didn't remember the date." I jumped and nearly fell off the platform. Mom never speaks that way to Aunt Doreen!

"Oh!" Aunt Doreen cried, and buried her face in her hands. "I can't believe it. I was truh-*trying* to do something good for Celeste, and look where it gets me." She sniffled loudly. Angelique reached around me, passing her a box of tissues.

Mom's face softened. She put an arm around her sister and patted her shoulder.

"It's okay, Doreen. I know you were just thinking of Celeste. And we're grateful. She'll be there. She will. There's plenty of time," my mother soothed. "The fashion show is in the morning, and the wedding doesn't begin until five. We'll be there in plenty of time. And," she said, offering a super wide Smile of Desperation, "her hair and makeup will already be done."

Oh, I thought. *I can do both.* I slumped. Visions of the Oreos waiting for me when I got home disappeared. The Negative Twenty settled on my back like a cloak.

It went on from there. Aunt Doreen was In A State, shaking her head and flailing her arms, worried that I'd miss my cousin's wedding. Mom pulled out every comforting word and calming gesture she knew to settle her down—probably wishing she'd never set her off in the first place. While they were distracted, Angelique nudged me and I slipped off the platform and into the dressing room. None too soon either, since I had to blow my nose and didn't think my sniffles would hold it that much longer.

I took my time changing, and by the time I went into the main part of the store, Mom and Aunt Doreen had worked things out.

"You need to just go to that pageant and make us proud," Aunt Doreen said, patting my cheek. "It'll be a great day for you *and* Kathleen when you win."

"No pressure," I said, searching for an escape. Angelique came to my rescue.

"Ze dress looks good," she said, gesturing to me. "It will be lovely when it's done."

Mom and Aunt Doreen nodded. "Beautiful," Mom acknowledged. "And the sleeves fit wonderfully."

"Absolutely," Aunt Doreen agreed.

Angelique smiled. From the front of the store, Kirsten called, "Mom . . . let's go. I've got practice in an hour."

The moms moved toward her voice. I started to follow, when I felt a bony hand on my shoulder and heard a low voice in my ear.

"I don't know what you're doing, girl, but I haven't touched ze sleeves. You keep it up and zis horrible dress will be as beautiful on you as eet can be." She released me and I left with a grin. The Negative Twenty felt lighter with every step. Maybe it was now the Negative Fifteen?

Chapter 18

ONCE RECOVERED FROM my cold, I resumed Operation Skinny Celeste. And with Millie and Katy keeping tabs on my calorie-burning activities, it gave me extra reasons to stick to my plan. Unfortunately, it was harder than I thought. I played ball with Ben once or twice after dinner, but I tired quickly and couldn't run for the ball fast enough to catch it if he tossed it over my head. It was like playing "pick up the ball" instead of "catch."

"I give up," I said to Millie at lunch one day. Sandra hadn't been to see us since the BBQ Day Bathroom Talk a week earlier. I'd taken to sitting with my back to Lively's table so I wouldn't have to watch Sandra tossing her hair and laughing with the rest of the ant-friends. And so every time she did, I wouldn't feel the stab in my heart. "It's not working. Ben pretended he couldn't find his glove last night when I asked him if he wanted to go outside." I pushed salad around with my fork.

"Maybe you need to do something a little less . . . athletic," she said, eyes on the table of boys across from us. She'd recently developed a crush on Mike Arroyo from our science class. He, at least, was much better than the so-called popular boys in our grade like Robbie Flan, Philip Mikowski, and the others who hung around with Lively. Mike was a great artist, and as far as I could tell spent most of his time drawing in a sketchbook—I'm not sure how Millie ever got a look at his face outside of classes, since all I ever saw was the top of his head or his doodles. But he never called me names, or pushed me in the hall. He usually ate with Alan Okuri and Brandon Cho, and all three of them were peering at his artwork.

"Like what?"

As though he felt her gaze, Mike shifted in his seat and glanced around the lunchroom.

"Well, my mom walks our dog with some of her friends," she said, bringing her attention to me in a hurry. "Just around the neighborhood. We could do that, if you want. Walking's not hard." The bell rang.

Walking I can do, I thought. *I'll only puff a little bit.* I said I'd try it out, and we stood to clear our garbage.

"Oops," came a snide voice from my left, and I was shoved toward the trash can. "'Scuuuse me."

"Knock it *off*, Lively," I said to her back as she wove through the end-of-lunch crowd. Sandra's brown ponytail bobbed in front of her, mocking me. I shook my head and dropped my crumpled napkin and milk carton into the garbage.

"Jerk," Millie muttered. "We should get Katy to figure out some fancy scientific way to get rid of her with no one knowing."

Seemed there was hope for the Secret Plot to Destroy Lively after all. "Great idea," I said, watching her bounce her way out of the caf with Philip Mikowski and her ant-friends. "Maybe she could put glue in Lively's lip gloss."

"Glue?" Millie asked.

I slung my backpack over my shoulder. "Yeah. It's the only way we'll get her to keep her mouth shut."

Millie's giggle followed me all the way to class.

When I got home from school, Mom was waiting for me in the kitchen with a cluster of brightly colored miniature shopping bags.

"I bought you some treats," she said as I dropped my backpack and went to the fridge for my now-standard after-school snack of an apple . . . although I did give the pantry door a longing look.

What now? I thought, imagining the horrible possibilities: an "I'm a HuskyPeach Teen Queen" T-shirt? A lifetime supply of chocolate cookies? Mom could do so much damage.

"Well," she said, smiling, "I've noticed that you've been enjoying more veggies and looking better. What's brought that on?" She waited for me to respond, but I didn't. After a few seconds, she continued. "As a reward, I picked up a few things and thought we could, you know, practice a little before we see Christian next weekend." She took bottles, brushes, and tubes from the bags.

"I was hoping you'd forget about next weekend," I muttered. How could using those bottles and tubes be fun?

Or a reward? *A new Theo Christmas download is a reward. A sundae is a reward. This is more Husky Torture.*

"Look—this one's liquid foundation, and this one is powder foundation. I bought some lipstick, and here's some different eye shadow combinations." The pile grew larger.

"Wow, Mom. Thanks. Um, you sure did buy a lot of stuff." Mom barely wore any makeup herself, just lipstick and some eye shadow when she and my dad went out to dinner. "Do *you* know how to use all this?"

"Well, I thought we could experiment. It'll be fun. And won't Christian be surprised when he sees you."

Shocked is more like it, I thought.

"I don't know, Mom. I mean, we can try it, but all of that really isn't me, you know?" Hoping that I could convince her to scale back, I tried one more approach. "Besides, Christian said I just needed 'enhancement.'"

"You'll like it, honey, you'll see. You didn't see him working on you. He used more than you think. Let's go into the bathroom. The light's better there."

There was no way to resist. I followed her into the bathroom and plunked down on the toilet seat lid. She lined up supplies on the counter, smoothed hair away from my face, and went to work.

A cold liquid slimed my cheeks. I squirmed. "I don't think he used anything cold, Mom," I said. She wiped it with a sponge.

"I'm evening your complexion. The woman at the counter said you need to start with an even complexion before you do anything else." She spread the cold stuff all over my face.

It does *wash off,* I reminded myself, and gave up making suggestions. As I opened, closed, lifted, and lowered, I imagined how glamorous I'd be when Mom was done. Maybe she was right. Maybe Christian rushed, and I needed more than he gave me. After all, I only had a few minutes with him. I imagined walking into Saturday's competition as Model Celeste already. He would be so proud. Erika would declare that since I was too thin and beautiful to be a HuskyPeach, they were moving me to the SkinnyBanana contest down the hall. *Then* they'd see "bubbly and engaging" Celeste!

Mom's humming brought me back to reality. "Almost done," she said, lunging at my eyelashes with a mascara wand. "Hmmm. Not quite the same look Christian gave you, though." She made one last swipe with the mascara and stepped back, studying the results. I sat straighter and presented my best Serious Model Face. The longer she examined me, the darker her eyes became. It was as though a little rain cloud blew across her face.

"Can I see?" I asked, hoping that her expression was due to the fact that her Little Girl looked All Grown-Up. She nodded.

I stood and turned to the mirror. Two weeks earlier, when Christian introduced me to the reflection of Model Celeste, I couldn't believe how great I looked. This time, I just couldn't believe *how* I looked.

Put it this way: If Christian's makeup job was like a soft candle flame, Mom's was harsh, tacky neon. He cast Spells of Beauty. Mom created a Clown Face Collage. The foundation was too light, turning my face a different color than my neck.

My cheeks were defined by a heavy pink diagonal stripe. My eyelashes looked good—she knew how to hold a mascara wand, at least—but the eye shadow was straight out of the Book of Black Eyes. She watched me studying their dark-ringed smudges.

"I was going for the smoky look," she said.

"Of course," I replied. The lipstick was too bright and a streak of it darted across my front teeth. Every smudge and smear accentuated my round cheeks, chubby chin, and fat neck.

"Let me get the remover." She sighed. "I never was any good at this."

"Maybe it's harder to do when it's not on yourself," I offered, fighting to keep my voice light. I dropped my eyes from the mirror. She returned with the remover and a handful of cotton balls and undid her spell. Real Celeste emerged from under the paint.

Mom tidied the bottles and tubes, dropping each into a bag as she did so. "Let's leave Christian to his own magic next Saturday," she said. "I'll put this in your room so you can try it on your own. Maybe you'll have better luck than me."

I eyed the bag. "Doubt it." *I'm a one-magician girl,* I thought. Once in my room, however, I stashed the bag with my Modeling Challenge materials. *Maybe Christian can teach me how to use it.*

Or at least tell you what to get rid of, Red Bathing Suit Woman finished.

Chapter 19

TRUE TO THEIR word—which was more than I could
say for Sandra, who completely stopped calling and didn't
seem interested in being Best Friends in school *or* out—Katy
and Millie met me to walk around the AlHo track each
afternoon over the weekend. Once I forced myself to get
over my memories of the Fitness Challenge and Yurk Fest
(and the fact that I still had Coach Anapoli's gift card in my
backpack), and Katy and Millie promised there would be
no running, everything went great. For two days, we met,
walked four laps, and went home. It tired me out, and I
huffed and puffed my way through the last lap, but I kept
reminding myself how many calories I was burning and
pictured the shrinking Negative Twenty. Mom and Dad,
who thought I was working with Katy and Millie on a school
project, were thrilled that I was getting together with other
kids since I hadn't seen much of Sandra lately. Thankfully,
Aunt Doreen's multiple wedding duties kept Mom busy and

prevented her from prodding about Sandra—or my "healthy choices"—too much. Mom was suspicious, though. I was grateful to escape her Questioning Eyebrows.

The third time, though, everything was different. I met Millie at the edge of the track after last period. We sat and waited for Katy to return from the high school. Her mom's car turned in to the parking lot.

"Ready to go?" Katy said, after exiting and walking over to us. Millie bent to tie her shoe. I nodded.

When Millie finished, we started our first lap.

"So, Millie, did you see Mike Arroyo looking at you in social studies today?" Katy began. I envied Millie's toffee skin. She didn't blush.

"Nooo. Was he? You'd better be telling the truth," she said. She stopped walking and fiddled with the string on her hoodie.

Must be nice to like someone without worrying about what they think of your look, I thought.

"C'mon," Katy said. "We need to keep going." She rolled her eyes at me, then tugged on Millie's arm to get her moving again.

"Tell me if it's true," Millie demanded, picking up speed. I huffed but kept up.

"Of course it is. Why would I lie? His brother is in chem with me in the afternoon. He's so good at balancing equations," she said. Did I see a dreamy smile flit across her lips? Before I could be sure, she continued, "Want me to ask him if Mike likes you?"

"No! Well, maybe . . . I don't know. Celeste, what do you think?" She turned to me for help.

It surprised me when Katy and Millie made room for me in their friendship. For so long, I had been part of a twosome—just me and Sandra—that I never thought three friends could work. It just didn't occur to me that they would need my opinion or advice on anything.

I grinned. "I don't know. What if his brother says something to him and then Mike gets nervous about it and doesn't want to talk to you? Maybe Katy should wait a week, and you try and talk to him in social studies or science a couple of times."

Millie nodded, considering my answer. We finished lap one. *This is so much better than gym,* I thought.

And so much better than listening to a certain Jolly Rancher-crunching girl's obsession with Robbie Flan, Red Bathing Suit Woman responded.

During lap two, we considered all the possible ways Millie could talk to Mike without making him suspicious: asking for homework, dropping something and asking him to pick it up, working in a group with him during class . . . there were endless options.

"Don't you have a dog?" I asked, remembering something Millie had said at lunch. "Mike draws dogs sometimes. I've seen his sketchbook. Maybe that's a way to start talking."

Katy and Millie shared a glance.

"Couscous is an interesting subject," Katy said, smirking. "Don't you think Mike'd want to draw him?"

Millie frowned. "I don't think that's the right conversation starter," she snapped. I was confused.

"What am I missing?" I fought to keep the Third-Wheel Whine out of my voice.

"It's a long story," Millie said. Her face smoothed back to its regular sunny smile.

"But a good one," Katy added, and giggled.

Millie scowled at Katy. "It happened last year," she began. We were just about to start lap three.

"Hold that thought—I have to go to the bathroom," I said.

"Want us to come with you?" Katy asked. I shook my head.

"I'll be right back. You can tell Katy all about our Secret Plot to Destroy Lively while I'm gone," I joked to Millie.

I stepped off the track and crossed the parking lot back to AlHo. With everyone gone, my footsteps echoed in the main hall. The first two girls' bathrooms I tried were locked, and I started to get desperate. I'd finished a bottle of water during my last class.

The H-wing bathroom—of the famous "best friends, outside of school" conversation—was unlocked.

As I finished in the last stall, the door squeaked open. Muffled crying filled the room. I sat back on the toilet, staring at my hands. It was embarrassing to listen in on someone else's problem. *I'll just slip out once whoever it is goes in a stall.*

A backpack zipper scratched, and after rummaging

through papers and books the crier found what she was looking for. Feeling brave, I peeked through the crack in the door to see who it was, but the person was just out of sight in the mirror. A cell phone beeped, and then Lively Carson's voice, snot-filled but clear, floated over the top of the stall. My heart froze as solid as a glacier. *What was she still doing at school?*

"M-Mom?" Lively said. "It's me. . . . No, no, I'm not hurt, but it's . . . it's terrible!" Lively started to sob, then ducked into a stall up the row. "You need to come get me!"

A team of sled dogs couldn't have pulled me from my stall. *What's so terrible about Lively Carson's life? Did she lose a barrette?* Eavesdropping embarrassment forgotten, I strained my ears and tried to quiet my breathing to hear every word.

"It *leaked*, Mom! It's leaking all over my shirt!"

What is she talking about?

"If anyone sees, they'll muh-muh-make fun of me!" She blew her nose in a great snotty burst. I cringed.

Lively Carson worries about people making fun of her? Who would dare?

"I tripped running for the bus and landed on a cuh-cuh-corner of my history book and it popped!" Lively was obviously having a hard time keeping in control. "And now I'm lopsided!" She wailed that last sentence.

Understanding washed over me. I almost choked because I forgot to breathe. Lively's perfect, perky, round figure was fake! Whatever she used to stuff her bra had sprung a leak.

Well that *certainly explains how they magically appeared after summer vacation this year,* Red Bathing Suit Woman sniffed.

"I told you not to put the water bras in the washing machine or dryer! You nuh-nuh-need to pick me up." A pause. "I don't care about the soccer game. Everyone will see!" She blew her nose again. "I hate soccer anyway."

She hates soccer . . . ? I thought. *Then what . . . ?* But Lively's conversation distracted me from going any further with that question.

"Put toilet paper in? Is that all you can think of? I can't do that! And my shirt is all wet." Another, longer pause. "Okay, fine. Four thirty. I have my sweater."

The conversation was ending. I had to get out of the bathroom before Katy and Millie sent a search party. Making only the tiniest movements, I crept from the stall. The door squealed and I stopped, holding my breath.

"Who's that?" Lively called, sniffing and trying to sound normal. "I heard you."

Please, please be too worried about your soggy boob to check. I forced my legs to work. Lively blew her nose a third time. I became a statue, counted to five, then pushed through the door to the hallway, heart pounding and sweating like it was lap three on Yurk Day.

Katy and Millie were sitting at the edge of the track when I arrived. Before they could even ask a question, the words poured from me.

"Oh my gosh, you wouldn't believe it . . . they're *fake!* The whole time, it's been a water bra and it *leaked* and now we *know* and I can't believe it . . ." They let me prattle like a lunatic for a minute or so, just watching me stand and sweat and talk.

"Um, Celeste?" Katy started, using a kind voice. She had twirled a blade of grass around her finger, the tip of which was now purple. She unwrapped the strand.

I nodded. "I mean, she was on the phone with her mom and she's all wet—"

"Celeste," Katy said again, firmer. "Stop and breathe."

I inhaled, then opened my mouth. "But you need to *know!*"

"Again," Katy said.

Inhale, exhale.

"Now talk," said Millie. "But tell us who—and what—you're talking about. It sounds awful."

"Lively!" I blurted. "She doesn't have—well, *anything!* She has a water bra!" I told them the whole story. By the time I finished, we were laughing hysterically.

"Oh boy," Katy said, wiping tears from her cheeks, "this is the best workout we've had all week. My stomach is going to be killing me tomorrow."

"You're luh-luh-*leaking!*" Millie squealed, pointing at Katy's tears. That set us off again.

Between gasping for air and wiping my own eyes, I thought, *Maybe we don't need Katy's science brain to develop a Secret Plot to Destroy Lively after all. Maybe she can do it on her own.*

Chapter 20

AS THOUGH SHE knew that something was up, Lively left the three of us alone for a few days. She wasn't nice, of course, but she didn't go out of her way to be mean. Mostly, she ignored us. It didn't matter, though. Every time I saw her I stifled a giggle. Once, Millie even made the water fountain squirt as she walked by. I leaned against the lockers, I was laughing so hard. Then it was time for gym class.

The Gift Card of Humiliation still taunted me from the bottom of my backpack. It had been nearly four weeks since Yurk Fest, and I hadn't been able to bring myself to give it to Coach Anapoli. The longer I waited, the worse it was. Her brown speckled sneakers were visible reminders of my explosive failure. *Why hadn't she bought herself a new pair?*

Coach grouped us into teams for a set of soccer games. I was on a team with Lively and Katy. Millie played against us, and Coach assigned Sandra to a different squad, which was fine by me. Her careful avoidance was getting old. The hurt was still there, but now it was a dull throb that flared up every so often—like when we were in places where we used to hang out, such as gym class.

Once we walked to the field and Coach led us through warm-ups, we split into groups to play.

"Great," Lively said once Coach was far enough away. "I got stuck with the bovine brigade." She rolled her eyes, mooed, and whinnied.

The familiar heat of shame crept over me as the other girls on the team laughed. The Negative Twenty plopped onto my shoulders. Next to me, Katy's face was still as stone.

"Jerk," she muttered. "And besides, genius, horses aren't bovines. They're equines."

We took our positions and started the game. I played goalie, since it didn't require me to run that much. Joanie Purcell, on Millie's team, slipped past Lively—who was busy checking her nail polish—and Heather Wilson's defense and slammed the ball past me, into the upper right corner of the net. I barely had time to react, let alone stop it.

When I bent to pick up the ball and toss it to the girls, Lively started in on me.

"You can't do anything right, you cow!" she said, furious. "You should've blocked it. You had time to get it." Speechless, I stood in the goal holding the ball.

"Knock it off," Katy said, jogging over from midfield. "If you had been playing defense Joanie couldn't have made that shot." Curious about the delay, Millie's team stopped celebrating and wandered to our side of the field. Lively had an audience.

"It's the goalie's job to block the shot. Cows shouldn't be allowed to play," Lively finished, hands on her hips.

Even as the heat of anger built up in me, I squeezed the ball to my chest to protect myself from her words. *Lively always gets away with this*, I thought. *Nothing makes her stop.*

Then I remembered: There *was* something that could get her to shut up forever . . . if I had the courage to do anything about it. Lively finished her tirade and the group broke up, meandering to their positions to resume the game. *Now or never.* I took a deep breath and squeezed the sides of the ball, elbows cocked.

"Hey, Leaky," I called. She spun in my direction. I faltered, but only for a second. *Be brave.*

"Not everyone is as perfect as you *think* you are. So back off." I heaved the ball as hard as I could at her chest. *Take that!* It flew straight and even, and I thought Lively was too surprised to catch it. At the last moment she did, though, and the loud slap that the ball made on her hands was the only sound on the field. She glared at me and I stared right back.

Nice shot! cheered Red Bathing Suit Woman. I hadn't wanted to hurt her, just scare her a little—or maybe cause the S.S. *Fakeboobs* to spring a leak.

"Good catch, Lively," Carlee Morgenstern said. Lively's Expression of Evil made Carlee step back.

"Cows don't throw hard," she said. But everyone had heard that slap.

I'm not afraid of you anymore, I thought. And the amazing thing was, it was true. Even more amazing? I think Lively knew it. Instead of making any more snarky comments, she turned, tucked the ball under her arm, and carried it out for the kickoff.

I let in two more goals, but Lively never said a word. And even though we lost 3–2, I went into the locker room feeling like a winner.

Chapter 21

SATURDAY ARRIVED TOO quickly. It was time for the next round of the Modeling Challenge: a practice session for the fashion show. Since Dad and Ben were at a Little League game and couldn't distract her, Mom followed me around the house while I got ready, closer than my shadow. Although not as anxious as I was two weeks before, I still had no desire to rush to the city and figure out how to purposely lose this round. Mom, though, was raring to go and full of speculation.

"What do you think you'll be wearing?" she asked as I dug through the pile of clean laundry on my bed, looking for a hoodie and another pair of track pants. The ones I'd put on earlier were a little loose, and I needed to see if it was my imagination. I shook my head.

"Dunno."

"I wonder if we'll be in the same group as last time," she said. "Or if they'll even have groups this week."

I wonder how long it will take me to go crazy from your questions, I thought, but I didn't say anything.

On the ride up, Mom started making Motherly Reminders: Sit up straight, look up and out when you walk, smile.

"What if they don't want me to smile? Or if they say I should slouch?" I asked, just to be annoying. "Should I still do it?"

"Do exactly what they tell you, Celeste. I'm just trying to help." She sounded hurt. I snuck a look at her. Hands tight on the wheel, forehead wrinkled, eyes locked on the road: She was nervous for me! My desire to annoy her flagged.

"Sorry, Mom. I guess I'm just anxious."

She offered me a big smile and patted my hand. "I know. It's okay. You'll do great. Dad and I are very proud of you."

The P-word again. Every time she said it, I felt terrible about what I was trying to do.

Do you want to win? Red Bathing Suit Woman's voice popped into my head. *'Cause you could try to do well today and become Miss HuskyPeach, if that's what you really, really want. Be a chubby teen queen for the world to see.*

That's enough! I told her. *I just want to be Celeste.*

When we reached PeachWear, our guide—appearing just as frazzled as last time—led us through the office building into an attached warehouse. The main level was a big open area with a concrete floor and no windows. Above us, the other levels consisted of walkways made of metal grates that wrapped around the inside edges of the building. Conveyor belts and tracks crisscrossed the center shaft.

A runway attached to a stage was set up in the middle of the room, surrounded by chairs. Stylists, contestants, and their moms bustled around racks of clothes and the perimeter. Brownie and cookie trays were sprinkled throughout. *Can't forget the snacks,* I thought with sarcasm. This time, thanks to all my work avoiding temptation, my tummy barely rumbled at the sight of them. Every whirring blow dryer and conversation was magnified and echoed around the room, competing with the sound of boxes and packages sliding along the conveyor belts.

"It's a little noisy," the guide said, practically yelling. "But this is the biggest space we own. This is our regional shipping warehouse. We didn't expect to be sending a shipment today. Another center flooded last night and the stores it supplies need stock." Mom struggled to look interested. I didn't bother pretending.

The guide continued. "We've set up styling stations to make things more comfortable." As she spoke, she walked around the stage at a brisk pace. I huffed a little, but discovered I was able to keep up. She led us to Christian.

As soon as he saw me and Mom, he put down his supreme-sized coffee and zipped over to dole out hugs. "Look who's here," he said. All my leftover anxiety and reluctance disappeared. I gave him a big smile.

Frazzled Guide made a clicking sound. "You've got thirty minutes," she said, checking her watch. "Then I'll take you to wardrobe." She scuttled off without waiting to see if we had questions.

"Well, let's get started," Christian said. "Although I don't think we'll need that much time." He winked and bent over his magic box.

While his back was to us, Mom gestured with the bag of makeup supplies we'd brought from home. "Ask him," she mouthed. I went from Calm and Comfortable back to Shy and Anxious.

"Um, Christian," I said. "I was wondering. I mean, if you have time, if you could show me how to . . . Last time, you said . . ." My words were as organized as his makeup toolbox.

He turned, pouffy brush in one hand, compact in another. "Absolutely. Like I said, it won't take long." He swished the brush in the powder and bent to apply it. I closed my eyes and waited. And waited.

What's wrong? I cracked my eyelids and peered out. Christian stood, brush poised and ready, eyes searching my face.

"Is everything okay?" Mom asked. That's when I opened my eyes all the way. My stomach tightened.

Christian blinked and straightened. "Fine. No problem," he said to Mom. "Your cheeks are different," he said to me with a raised eyebrow. "Your face is thinner."

My heart bounced into my throat. I struggled with shock and put on my Innocent Expression. *Negative Twenty? What Negative Twenty?*

"Really?" I kept my voice as even as I could, but I wanted to dance, leap, and sing. Operation Skinny Celeste was working!

"I thought so." Mom's smile was smug.

Christian nodded and raised his brush. "Close your eyes,"

he directed. The soft bristles tickled my cheeks. "See? Her cheekbones and chin are more defined."

"She's been working hard," Mom said in response. Beneath my closed lids, I rolled my eyes.

After that, it was back to Christian's Magic Show. A purse, pucker, and turn later, I was transformed. This time I paid special attention: There was no cold, slimy sponge-stuff smeared on my face.

"All set," he said, offering me his hand mirror with a flourish. "Even more fabulous than before, if I may be so bold."

This time, I reached for it without hesitation. Christian was right: Model Celeste was back, but better. He'd highlighted my cheeks, and for the first time I could see the changes he saw in the mirror. My face, which had been round, round, round like the rest of me, had a slight oval shape to it now. My chin, which had been hard to pick out between my neck and my cheeks, was defined. I grinned.

"Thank you," I said.

"She's beautiful," Mom said. I'd forgotten she was there.

"Now, about your lessons," Christian said, glancing at his watch. "We have plenty of time, so I'm going to—"

"Oh good," Frazzled Guide interrupted. Her hair, smoothed into a neat bun when we arrived, had come loose and stray tendrils haloed her head. "You're done. We're late. You need to get to wardrobe right now."

"But you said—" I began.

"But it's not—" Christian started.

"But we're—" Mom tried.

"Scheduling problem," she replied, cutting us off with a wave of her hand. "Someone was accidentally left out; we have to push everything up a few minutes to make room. Let's go," she directed.

My heart gained all the weight my face had lost. *His magic only goes so far,* I thought. I slid out of the chair. Christian gave me a squeeze and a warm grin. "There's always next time," he said. "Go out there and wow them."

I tried to smile. Mom said good-bye and we followed Frazzled Guide through the crowd to our next stop. As we walked, I watched other contestants being primped, moms hovering, and the packages on the upper levels of the warehouse sliding along the conveyor belts to their destinations.

On our way we saw Erika. On crutches. My face burned.

"How are you?" Mom asked, her face a reflection of my humiliation.

"Sprained," Erika replied, packing the word with accusation.

"I-I-I'm so sorry," I stammered, not able to meet her eye. "I feel—"

She tucked a crutch under her arm and waved me off. "I'll be fine in another week or two, they think."

"We need to go," Frazzled Guide interrupted, pointing at her watch.

"Don't be late on my account," Erika said.

By the time we reached the makeshift wardrobe department on the other side of the room, I had counted six snack tables of cookies and brownies. My tummy was back to its rumbling self, even with Christian's compliment.

Frazzled Guide stopped in front of a short chubby woman with wavy brown hair, rosy cheeks, and a wide smile. "Elsa, this is Celeste. She's number"—she ran her finger down a sheet of paper taped to a rack of clothes—"eleven."

Elsa nodded and placed a strong hand in the middle of my back. "Welcome to the HuskyPeach."

Mom moved to the rack of clothes and fingered some of the dresses and skirts. Our guide tried to smooth her hair back into its bun.

"Okay. We start in"—another check of the watch—"twenty minutes. Celeste, once you're finished with Elsa, please go directly to Staging Area Three." She pointed clear across the warehouse. "I'll be there with the group to give you instructions about the next part of the process." She stepped away from us, then spun and returned before we could move. "Sorry. Nearly forgot. Once you're in your PeachWear show clothes, we ask that you refrain from eating or drinking. You may have clear liquids, like water. If you want anything else, please get it now."

So they do have snack limits, I thought. "Thanks. I'm all set."

Frazzled Guide spun away again. A long strand of dark hair unmoored from her bun and drooped to her shoulder. She gave it an angry swipe as she strode to her next contestant.

"Looks like she's on her way to falling apart," Mom muttered.

"On her way?" Elsa asked. "I bet she's hiding behind the racks before today's over." She put her hands on her hips and turned to me. "Number eleven, right?" When I nodded, she said, "I have just the thing for you. Wait here." She disappeared into the clothing rack maze.

Mom put her arm around me and squeezed my shoulder. "You are so beautiful, honey. I can't wait to see what Elsa has in store for you."

Torn between feeling guilty and proud, I lowered my eyes to my feet.

Mom dropped her arm and scanned the room, a distracted expression on her face. "I shouldn't have had one of Christian's coffees after that bottle of water in the car," she said, eyes darting around the space. "I really have to go to the bathroom. Did you see one when we came in?"

"No," I answered, "but I'm sure you can ask one of the guides. There's one over there." I pointed at a petite blond woman in SkinnyBanana black.

"Will you be okay?" Mom asked. She shifted back and forth while waiting for my response.

"Yeah," I said. Elsa emerged from the maze, a bundle of burnt orange fabric wrapped in her arms as a prize. Mom bolted.

"Is something wrong?" Elsa asked. Arms full, she nudged me in the direction of a black fabric makeshift dressing room cubicle.

"Just looking for the bathroom," I responded. I stopped in front of what I assumed was the door—a piece of cloth tied back with a red ribbon.

"Oh." Elsa shook her head. "She'll be a while. There's only one women's bathroom on this level, and there was a line when I was there. And it's on the other side of the building."

Hope she gets back in time, I thought, my nerves acting up.

You're awfully nervous about a contest that you don't want to win, Red Bathing Suit Woman said. *Or have you changed your mind? Have a brownie.* I frowned at her.

"Here's your gown. There's a shopping bag on the floor of the changing room for your clothes. You did bring your own shoes, right?" I raised my bag. "Good, good," she said.

Another guide appeared with Ashley Freeman and her mom. They were wearing less makeup this week. I guess their stylist had taught them some tricks as well. Ashley grinned.

"You look great!"

"Thanks," I replied. "You too." She'd traded the Purple Bell-Sleeved Shirt of Awkwardness for a sleeveless blue dress that brought out her eyes.

"Heard about what happened with Erika last week," Ashley continued, her voice lowered. "Are you okay?"

I studied her face. Was she making fun of me? No, I decided. She was genuinely concerned.

"I'm fine . . ."

Her mom nudged her before I could say more. "Ash-*ley*, don't make friends with the competition." Ashley rolled her eyes.

Ashley's guide waved at Elsa, as if to hurry her along.

"In with you, then," Elsa said to me. "When you're done, come find me and I'll make any adjustments. It shouldn't need much—we took your measurements right off your application." She thrust the dress at me and went to help Ashley, whose mother tugged her away to what she probably considered was a "safe distance" from the competition.

I pushed my way into the changing room. The bulky dress was hard to see around, and the black fabric walls didn't help. I ended up running into the clothes hanger pole. It wobbled, but didn't fall over. *Don't need another disaster,* I thought. *I can take care of losing just fine.* I looped the hanger over the hook and finally got a good look at my attire for the day: a ball gown.

A big skirt, made of some shiny fabric that I didn't recognize, fanned to the floor. The rich orange color resembled fire. The top was trimmed with clear beads that I knew would sparkle under the lights on the stage. Oddly, though, the straps that held the dress to the hanger were made of thin white cotton strings—not even close to matching the rest of it. *It's probably part of the "look,"* I thought. Outside of the Modeling Challenge, there'd be no way I'd wear it—too scratchy, too revealing, too . . . *much. But, according to my mother, what do I know?* One thing I *did* know: There was no way those flimsy straps would hide my blue and white floral bra. I'd have to go free-style.

Fan-tastic, I thought, and scowled. I piled my clothes into the shopping bag (printed with a bold HuskyPeach emblem), and once standing in my "unmentionables," as Grandma called them, I realized that I was not entirely comfortable taking my bra off in the makeshift changing room. The solution to my problem came straight out of Coach Anapoli's gym class: Put the dress on first and pull the bra out second.

Do I step into it? I thought, studying it on the hanger. I didn't see how I could. Instead, I dug under the hem, through the irritating tulle, to find the opening. Swimming up through layers of fabric, I tugged the whole thing over my head. When my head and shoulders cleared the top of the dress, I peered down at where the straps should've been, to loop my arms through.

"Hi there," came Elsa's voice through the curtain and over the clamor of the warehouse, "do you need help with the zipper or anything?"

Zipper? What zipper? My hands flew across the top of the dress, patting and searching for seams. Couldn't find one. *Oh no. Did I wreck it?*

"Uh, no? No. I'm okay. Thank you," I said, trying to sound convincing and quiet my slamming heart.

"Just give a holler if you need me," she said. I waited until I was sure she was gone before I moved again.

Please, please don't let it be ruined, I thought. This time, I reached around to the back of the dress. And felt the zipper seam that split it from the top to below the waist. It was still closed, and I couldn't feel any tears around it. *Phew.* My heart slowed down. I returned to dealing with the straps.

It was then I realized that I had two very large problems. One, those little white string things weren't straps. They were teeny loops that kept the dress on the hanger. And two? The top was too big.

Okay, I had three problems. The third? The only items qualified to hold up my Giant Gown of Fire were my hands, clenched firmly at the top of the dress.

Chapter 22

HOW CAN I walk down a runway like this? What if they want me to hold something? I spun in a circle, hoping I missed a crucial accessory—like suspenders. No luck. Next, I actually spun the dress itself. On me. It was large enough that all I had to do was lift my arms and I could slide it around. No hidden straps, buttons, zippers, or ties that I could see. *I'd even settle for staples,* I thought.

This is what it's like to be skinny, Red Bathing Suit Woman whispered to me. *Isn't it nice to have something not fit—and have it be too big?*

Knock it off, I responded. *This is what it's like to be panicked.* This was a certifiable Aunt Doreen Moment: I was shaking, sweating, and if I had anyone to talk to, there'd be screeching.

In a moment of clarity, I remembered: *Elsa. Elsa can fix it. She can make adjustments.* I looped the handles of my shopping bag over one arm, clutched the top of the dress, and pushed out of the clothing curtain.

Elsa's Rack Maze stood to my right. The spot where Elsa met me and the other contestants was empty. *She's probably getting someone a dress.* I waited, guides scooting back and forth with moms and girls. Elsa still didn't come back.

Instead, a loud horn tooted, silencing the chatter and freezing everyone where they stood. A voice blared over the PA system.

"Walk-through begins in five minutes. I repeat, five minutes. All contestants, please report to your staging area. Parents and stylists, take your seats."

Like everyone else, I went into Full-Blown Panic mode. Only, instead of trying to primp or smooth for one last time, I fled. *Have to find help,* I thought. *Have to find help,* over and over again.

Every guide I tried to stop waved me in the direction of the staging areas. "Just go there," they said. I headed in the direction of Staging Area Three, still clutching my dress top and shopping bag. As I crossed the big room, a flash of scarlet caught the corner of my vision. I stopped and turned my head to see my Gateway to Freedom: a big red EXIT sign.

I'll go out, change, sneak into the seats, and deal with Mom later. My heart pounded as hard as it had the day of the Fitness Challenge, and *that* had not ended prettily. Without another thought, I headed straight for the door.

Just a few more steps, I thought. *Almost there.* And then I was. It was a big steel door with a push bar across it, like the caf doors at school. As I reached for the bar with one hand (the other still holding up my gown), it jerked. I almost let go of the dress in surprise.

The door swung open, and I nearly crashed into Violet Page, who was trying to get in as fast as I was trying to get out. She was wearing track pants and a hoodie. *One more reason to be jealous of her.*

"Whoa," she said, waving a hand around her head. I caught a whiff of cigarette smoke. "Where are you going?"

The heat coming off my face could have melted metal. I gave her what I'm sure was a pathetic look—I didn't even have to try—and gestured at my dress with my chin.

"It, uhh, doesn't fit, and I couldn't find anyone to help me," I said.

"Too big?"

I nodded.

"Okay. We don't have much time." She tugged my elbow and led me back into the warehouse. Later, I realized that she didn't even ask why I was *leaving* the building to get help.

She stopped one of the petite guides. "Hey—I need your binder clip." Violet removed it from the pile of papers the woman was carrying and sent her on her way. "Skinny thing—have a sandwich," she muttered at her retreating black back. I giggled and Violet gave me her attention.

"This is an old trick," she said, guiding me to the side and out of traffic. "Put your arms up." When I hesitated, she frowned at me. "Look, I don't care what your girls are doing in there. I'm just going to make sure they continue to do it in private."

I raised my arms without a word. She didn't let the dress fall, but slid behind me and grabbed the extra fabric. Then she folded and rolled it. I heard a click and felt cold metal between my shoulder blades. Then came the sound of tape being pulled from a dispenser. I strained to see over my shoulder.

"Double-stick," she said, pulling a few inches off the roll. "I always keep it in my purse. Trick of the trade." She peeled the backing off, slid her hand inside my dress, and stuck the tape to my side. Then she pressed the fabric to my skin. Before I had time to be surprised that someone I barely knew was putting tape all over me, she was done. None too soon either.

"Attention, contestants. Two minutes to the show. Please report to your staging area," the voice boomed. "Violet Page, please report to the judges' table."

"Arms down," Violet said. She moved and stood in front of me. "Gotta go. This will hold you up fine. Just don't put your arms over your head and you'll be all set. Good luck. You look great." She jogged in the direction of the stage.

"There you are." Frazzled Guide appeared at my elbow. "We've been looking all over for you. You missed our group's walk-through. We're late. Can you listen and walk?"

I nodded, arms clasped to my sides, shopping bag of clothes I'd rather be wearing bumping against my knees.

"Each contestant comes onstage, goes down to the end of the runway, pivots, and comes back. The next contestant starts when the one before her finishes her pivot. So you'll pass someone on the way out and back. Got it?"

"Uh-huh," I said through clenched teeth. I was afraid that the dress would fall if I even opened my mouth. *Why did Violet have to be coming in right then?*

"Violet is going first, then we're up," Frazzled Guide said. Her bun was a bird's nest mess at the back of her head. We'd arrived at our staging area, where I saw Gail for the first time that day. Wearing an eggplant and electric blue dress—with enviable thick straps—she looked gorgeous, but terrified.

"So glad you're here," she whispered.

"Really?" I said before I could stop myself. Gail had been so quiet during the previous session, I had no idea if she liked me or not. She nodded her head.

"You're one of the most normal ones here. Everyone else is so . . . pageant-ized." Her description made me laugh. Frazzled Guide, however, wasn't in the mood for humor or conversation in her group.

"Get in line behind Ashley," she directed me, silencing Gail with a wave. "Remember: You go out when she finishes her spin. Girls!" She raised her voice to get everyone's attention. "The judges will be evaluating you on poise, confidence, and attractiveness. So walk pretty and smile big!"

A dance remix of "Dreaming Without You" blared through the building's speakers, covering the hum of the conveyor belts and sliding packages, soothing me even though its familiar melody had been amped up. Theo Christmas can make any bad situation better. An announcer's voice welcomed everyone to the second round of the PeachWear Modeling Challenge.

"Before we begin, Violet Page, our celebrity judge and former PeachWear model, will show our contestants what's expected of them." The announcer's voice faded and the volume of the music rose.

A kernel of excitement formed in the midst of my dress-related anxiety. It's not every day you get to see a real model strut the catwalk.

In a warehouse, under bright lights, Red Bathing Suit Woman added.

You're just jealous, I responded. *No matter how good your diet drink is, you're still stuck in a crumpled advertisement in last month's trash.* There was nothing she could say to that one.

The stage entrance was to our right. Violet appeared, wearing a silver evening gown that hugged every one of her ample curves. *How had she changed so quickly?* Her gray eyes reflected green in the light, and her flawless skin glowed. She smiled in our direction, then stepped up to the runway.

Ashley gripped my arm. "She's gorgeous!" she whispered. Her voice was so light and airy, I almost didn't hear her. I glanced at her: eyes wide, face slack, she was locked on to Violet Page like a missile to its target.

And she was. Violet the Model was nothing like the almost-bored, always-flaky judge from the previous session. This person was focused, direct, and sexy. She walked with a determined stride, peering at the audience from under narrowed lids. She kept her mouth pursed for the trip to the end of the runway. Mid-spin, she paused and flashed a dazzling smile. It was then that I realized: Her looks were only part of what made Violet beautiful. Confidence took care of the rest.

"Whoa," Ashley said as Violet returned, cheeks flushed and still beaming.

"Amazing," I agreed.

"I don't know if I can do that," said Gail. Her plump cheeks darkened. For those few minutes, I hadn't even been thinking about my turn. Anxiety tightened its coil in my middle.

"You'll be okay," said Ashley, sounding nervous too. At least she was trying to make Gail feel better. My tongue was cemented to the roof of my mouth.

The announcer came on again.

"Our first group is modeling our line of Occasions formalwear. Perfect for weddings, proms, or other social events, these fanciful frocks make any gathering festive."

Frazzled Guide gave Gail a shove toward the stage. The warehouse lights wouldn't go down, so the runway and audience were clearly visible. When Violet was up there, she was so magnetic, I hadn't even noticed. It took both me and Gail about the same amount of time to realize that this was a bad, bad thing. Onstage, everyone could see us, and we could see them. She stepped out, then froze, staring at the crowd.

"Gail, go!" hissed our guide. "Move it. Now!" Gail blinked when she heard her name, then bolted down the runway. So not like Violet. Her chest heaved with the effort of moving at high speed. I could sympathize. At the end of the ramp, she spun faster than a washing machine—so quick, even Frazzled Guide reacted slowly. She pushed Ashley up the stairs as Gail was on her way back. She passed me, shaking and sweating. I don't even think she remembered I was there.

Ashley, ever Mommy's pageant darling, walked slower than Gail, but she was nervous too. Her expression consisted of the biggest, fakest smile I'd ever seen, and every two steps she'd bring her right hand to her mouth, chew her nails, then drop the hand back to her side, giving her nerves away. Then it would happen again. After watching Violet's walk, I could imagine what her mom would say on the ride home. By the time she made her spin, I felt so sorry for her, I forgot I was next. And I forgot to worry about the dress.

"Go!" A shove and I was onstage.

I tried to smile, but all I could manage was a weak lift of the corners of my mouth. I spotted Christian in the audience, who gave me a big thumbs-up. Next, I saw Mom. She waved her arms like crazy. I couldn't even blink, I was so freaked out. Ashley and I passed each other—I caught her wide, terrified smile—and I made it down the runway and through my turn at the end. I grinned at the achievement.

Almost done, almost done, I thought, relieved that I hadn't tripped or fallen. I too had given up hope of re-creating Violet's walk. *At least I don't have to do anything on purpose to lose this round. I probably look like a toy soldier.* My arms stayed stuck to my sides. My face was as wooden as Pinocchio's.

The next contestant, Bay-be—Violet Page Explainer Mom's daughter—was about to pass me. She offered the crowd a huge smile and walked with her head up and shoulders back, just like Violet.

How is she so— but I didn't get to finish my thought.

Over the heavy dance music came a shout, loud and clear: "Look out!"

I stopped and tilted my head to the rafters and conveyor belts. A big brown box was plummeting straight toward me. Without thinking, I threw my arms over my head for protection.

The binder clip popped.

The tape tore.

The dress came down.

For a split second, I was aware of a breeze across my now-exposed top, then the box crashed onto my head, knocking me to the floor. It ripped, contents flying everywhere—bras.

Of course, I had time to think, just before I lost consciousness.

Chapter 23

ALTHOUGH I *WANTED* to die after the Top-Dropping Bra Bombing, I didn't. I wasn't even unconscious for long. As a matter of fact, the doctor said that I didn't even have a concussion. Unfortunately, I am sturdier than my little brother. Wrapping my head in my arms had protected me from harm, but not embarrassment. When I came to, I was face up in a pile of black lace Night Vixen double Ds.

The short version of what followed: humiliating transportation to the PeachWear offices, where I insisted on changing into my own clothes and they begged us not to sue; a trip to the emergency room, where at least four doctors and nurses asked why a box of bras had fallen on my head; and a long ride home during which Mom tried to explain that no one saw my "assets" because I was facing the stage, not the audience.

"And besides," she said, "they were too busy watching the box fall to notice anything else."

That did not make me feel better.

"I'm done," I told her, wincing and holding an ice pack to my head. "No more HuskyPeach for me. I'm not going back." I swiped at tears of anger and embarrassment. My head was killing me, I'd just flashed tons of people, and I hadn't eaten an Oreo in a month. Even Red Bathing Suit Woman knew enough to keep quiet.

When we got home, I went straight upstairs, passing a very confused-looking Dad and Ben in the kitchen.

"Why are you crying?" Ben called after me. "Did they do your hair wrong?"

There was no need for that.

"Because everything's awful—including you!" I shouted, pounding upstairs to my room.

I threw myself on the bed and cried into my pillow. I wept over the Bra Bombing, flashing everyone, and the whole horrible day. Big tears darkened my pillowcase. *Even my tears are fat*, I thought, followed by, *Why does Theo have to see me like this?* He politely stared over my head, ignoring my outburst. For some reason, this made me sob more. I had been trying so hard, and nothing worked out right. *I can't even lose the contest the way I want to.* Giving up cookies, eating salad for lunch, walking—those things hadn't made much difference. I was still fat enough to be a HuskyPeach, still best-friendless, still embarrassed, and still discouraged. I didn't even care what my tears were doing to Christian's magic makeup job, I just shuddered and sniffled snot.

When I finally stopped, my pillow was soaked, my makeup was smeared, and I was exhausted. It felt as though my insides had been hollowed out with Mom's melon baller.

I snuck into the bathroom to wipe my eyes and wash my face, avoiding the mirror the entire time. Then I went back to my room, avoiding everyone else. I didn't even glance at Theo before I crawled under the comforter.

Later, Millie or Katy called to see how the day went. I pretended to be asleep when Dad brought the phone into my room. "She's pretty worn out," he whispered before closing the door. I fell asleep for real then, because when I woke up it was dark out and everyone was in bed. *This day is finally over*, I thought, changing into my pajamas.

I didn't think it was possible, but I slipped beneath the covers and slept again.

Over the course of the week, I revealed to Katy and Millie what had happened during round two. Telling the story in small chunks was easier. They were just as horrified as I was mortified, which helped—even though Millie broke into fits of giggles every time she saw a cardboard box.

On Wednesday, to my surprise, Ashley and Gail IM'ed me to see how I was doing.

> Xmasgrl: OK, I guess. Headache gone.
> Wu-wu211: r u coming back?
> Xmasgrl: no way!!!!
> Ashfree: u should. We'll miss u!

It was nice of them to check in, but I couldn't imagine going back there. I was done with the HuskyPeach. Not everyone was getting the picture, though.

Millie called Friday afternoon. "You know, I was thinking. Since you might not finish the Challenge—"

"I'm *definitely* not going to," I interrupted.

"Okay, *definitely* not going to—you'll never get that help from Christian. What are you going to do with that makeup your mom bought?"

I hadn't thought about it. "Don't know, don't care," I said, eyeing a bag of Oreos Ben must have left on the kitchen counter. I'd stuck to Operation Skinny Celeste since the top-dropping—out of habit, I guess—but they were calling me.

"Your mom bought lots of stuff," Millie said. "You may as well use it. Why don't you come over tomorrow and bring it? Let's try it."

"You just want to look good for Mike," I teased. Millie had spoken to him every day before social studies—starting by asking if he had a pencil—and once or twice before science, and although there had been no confirmation from his brother through Katy that he liked her, she was hopeful.

"Not at all," she said, using a very prim voice. "I'm just trying to make sure that a friend's mom didn't waste her money." Then she laughed.

I agreed to come over, and we set a time. When I hung up the phone, I noticed an Oreo in my left hand. *How did you get there?* I asked it.

You picked it up, responded Red Bathing Suit Woman. *Didn't you like it when Christian said your face looked thinner? Is that cookie going to taste better than those words felt?*

The contest is over, I responded. *I don't need to lose any more.*

You might not need to, but do you want *to?* she asked. *There's nothing that says you have to stop.*

And no one to tell me I have to continue, I reminded her.

It's never been about anyone else, she pointed out. *This is about you, Celeste.*

I flipped the Oreo over and over in my hand. Dark chocolaty crumbs dotted my fingers.

I'm not a contestant anymore. Things are the way they used to be.

Not exactly. You might not be a contestant, Red Bathing Suit Woman said, *but you're still a HuskyPeach.*

I scowled. My *"appetite for life" is getting smaller every day, hanging around you.* Before she could say another word, I tossed the cookie in the garbage, grabbed an apple from the fridge, and went to my room.

The next morning, Dad dropped me off at Millie's brown and white house. I'd never been there before and felt shy ringing the bell.

"Hi, Mrs. Taposok," I said when her mom opened the door. "Is Millie home?" A "yip-yip" noise came from somewhere inside. I must have looked surprised at the sound, because Mrs. Taposok laughed.

"You must be Celeste. That's Couscous, our Chihuahua. You'll meet him in a sec."

Couscous is a Chihuahua?

"And call me Mrs. T. Everyone does." Mrs. T had a wide smile, like Millie, and the same thick dark hair. When I stepped inside, I could smell something delicious coming from the kitchen.

"Millie," her mom called down a hall, "Celeste is here. She'll be right out," she said to me. "She's taking care of the dog."

I nodded. For some reason I pictured Millie's family having a bigger dog.

"Millie showed me your school picture. Have you . . . gotten taller since then? You look wonderful." She fiddled with the white dishcloth in her hand. *Same way Millie does with her hoodie,* I noticed.

My smile came close to knocking my ears off. "Thank you. I don't think so," I replied, ignoring a smirking Red Bathing Suit Woman. I didn't have to say anything else, because Millie came down the hall, holding a small beige dog with short hair and big ears and eyes, wearing a pink tee.

"Couscous, Celeste," she said. The dog cocked his head at me and yipped.

"Is he all set?" Mrs. T asked. Millie put him down and he sniffed my shoes.

"Think so. I squeezed four times to make sure." Her answer satisfied Mrs. T, because she nodded.

"Squeezed?" I said, trading shyness for curiosity.

Mrs. T turned to me. "There was an accident last year. Francisco—Mr. T—backed over Couscous when he was leaving for work. He loves that dog. It devastated him. We thought Cousie wouldn't be able to walk again. Luckily, the only problem was some nerve damage." Her eyes welled up with tears talking about it.

"It's okay, Mom," Millie jumped in. "Couscous is fine," she said to me. "He just can't feel when he needs to, you know—go. And even if he could, he can't. The nerves don't work."

"He needs to be squeezed," Mrs. T finished. "Over the toilet. Francisco usually does it when he's home, but he's out running errands this morning. We all take turns."

"Oh," I said, and nodded like I understood. "You need to squeeze him." *This must've been the story she and Katy were going to tell me the day we found out about Lively's leaky boobs.*

"Yes," Mrs. T said. "Every four hours, just to be on the safe side. But if he eats cheese—"

"Let's go to my room," Millie interrupted. Her mom told us to let her know if we needed anything and said she'd be in the kitchen, wrestling a chicken. Couscous trotted after her.

"She's making rellenong manok, Filipino stuffed chicken, for my aunt's birthday dinner tonight," Millie explained. "It's really good, but complicated."

"Smells great," I said, puzzling over how, exactly, one squeezed a dog over a toilet. I'd have to ask Millie about it later.

Once in Millie's pink and white bedroom, we spread the makeup across her bed and cranked Theo Christmas on the stereo. She found a hand mirror, tissues, and remover, and we started our own primp session. I tried as best I could to explain what I thought Christian had done to me. I knew there was no liquid foundation involved, so we scooted that to one side. We used the big brushes, powder, blush, and eye shadow. Through trial and error, we discovered that certain shades of red didn't look right on Millie.

"Your skin almost turns greenish when this stuff is on it," I said, wiping a blush called Canyon Rose off her cheeks. Her bedroom door opened.

"That's because her skin has yellow tones in it," said Katy, followed by Couscous. "The yellow in the blush brings out the yellow in her skin. You'll look better if your blush has more brown in it," she directed to Millie. "Try another color."

"Hey," Millie said, and hopped off the bed to give Katy a hug. "I didn't even hear the bell. When did you get here?"

"Couple of minutes ago. Your mom let me in. Celeste, scoot over."

I cleared space for her on the bed. Although I liked Katy and was happy to see her, I was annoyed that Millie invited her without telling me. *Because Millie can only be friends with you now?* Red Bathing Suit Woman asked. I inhaled.

"We're trying the stuff my mom bought," I explained.

"Katy's kind of a makeup whiz too," Millie said to me. "I hope you don't mind that I invited her over, but I thought she might be able to help out."

"Really?" I couldn't have been more surprised if I found out that Katy juggled knives and ate fire. "But you don't wear any." I couldn't think of a time when I'd seen her in so much as lip gloss.

Katy shrugged. "When you have two older sisters who use you as their practice dummy before dances, dates, and proms, you learn a few things." She picked up a tube of mascara. "Plus, there's a science to this."

For the next hour we dabbed, brushed, lined, glossed, and sang along to Theo while Couscous slept on a—what else?—pink pillow in the corner. One of Mom's purchases turned out to be the perfect blush for Millie—Chocolate Berry—and the Granny Smith eye shadow made Katy's eyes light up as green as the bottom lens in a traffic light. However, nothing seemed right for me. The black mascara was too dark, the Canyon Rose blush too bright, the Jack Frost eye shadow too pale.

"This stuff isn't even close to the colors you need," Katy said in frustration, tossing a brush onto the comforter. "You need to go shopping. Ask Christian what he thinks you should buy, then I'll show you how to use it."

I almost agreed with her, then stopped. "No way," I said. "I'm done with HuskyPeach." The shame and hurt from the week before crept back. To distract myself, I gathered the makeup they didn't want and dropped it in the bag. The once shiny bottles and tubes were dull and used. Millie and Katy shared a glance. Couscous, awakened from his nap, stretched and trotted to the bed. I picked him up.

"Don't squeeze him," Katy reminded me. She didn't have to worry.

"Celeste," Millie said. "We know that what happened last week was really, really awful. But you look so good. It's only one more time."

Her words caught me off guard. Tears burned my eyes. I blinked and shook my head, afraid that I'd cry if I tried to talk. I stroked Couscous's head instead. It wasn't about looking good. After what Christian did to me, I knew I could look better. What was more important was that I wanted to look better—but on my own terms; not because I was fat or thin, but because I was me. This was about not wanting to be a HuskyPeach Chunky Teen Queen in front of the world. Before the contest, Fat Celeste had been left alone by almost everyone. Now, it seemed, no one wanted to leave me alone.

Or, I thought, *they don't want to leave the idea alone—this idea of me as someone I'm not.* A heavy blanket wrapped around my heart. Couscous licked my hand in sympathy, and Theo sang about love and loss from the speakers.

"Think about it," Katy said. "And if you don't want to finish it, that's fine with us." Millie nodded. "But if you want to, and you still want to work on Operation Skinny Celeste, we'll help you out. Okay?"

"Okay," I said, staring at the dog. "Thanks."

I knew they wanted to help, but the idea of being in front of all those people again made my belly flip. I'd finally convinced Mom to stop encouraging me to go back; I hadn't expected Millie and Katy to say anything about it.

The doorbell dinged. "That's my dad," I said, glancing at Millie's bedside clock. I handed Couscous to Katy.

"Will you think about it?" Millie asked, walking me to the front door.

"Yeah," I said. But I was thinking this: *Never again.*

"Were you expecting anyone?" Dad asked as we pulled into the driveway.

"Huh?" I said, still thinking about what Katy and Millie said. I followed his pointing finger. A blue mountain bike leaned against the side of the garage. Only one person had that bike and left it in that exact spot when she came over: Sandra.

What is she doing here?

Chapter 24

"THAT'S SANDRA'S BIKE, right?" Dad said, shutting the car off. "Did you know she was coming over?"

I shook my head, stunned. A thousand scenarios blew through my mind: She was there to apologize, she heard about the Challenge and was there to make fun of me in person, it was someone else's bike—and on and on. We hadn't talked since that day in the bathroom four weeks ago. The fun I'd had with Katy and Millie disappeared and anxiety took its place. Instead of Three Musketeers, I was facing this as a Lonely Only.

"Let's see what she's up to," Dad said. He opened the car door and got out. "It's been a while since she's been around."

Glued to my seat, I didn't move.

"Come on, Celeste. You can't stay in there. Are you okay?"

I nodded. He was right. My brain knew I couldn't stay there and I had to see what Sandra wanted. My insides, however, disagreed completely. As I stepped out of the car, my stomach churned, my palms started to sweat, and an old sock replaced my tongue. I forced myself to enter the house.

Sandra sat at our kitchen table, an open bag of chocolate chip cookies, a pile of crumbs, and a half-empty glass of milk spread in front of her. Those cookies were never so unappealing. Mom stood.

"Hi, honey," she said. "Sandra stopped by to see you."

"Hey," I croaked through my dry throat. I cleared it and tried again. "Hey." That time it sounded better. Mom didn't think so. She gave me her Be More Gracious eyebrow lift, which is one step below the Behave Yourself, Young Lady glare.

"Hi, Sandra," Dad said. "Haven't seen you in a while. How're things? How're your brother and sister?"

"Good, Mr. Harris," she responded, then swigged her milk. She was wearing a Lively Special: blue skirt, blue and white tank, blue sneakers, and—of course—sparkly blue earrings. *Did she pick her outfit to match her bike?* I wondered.

After a couple of minutes of small talk (during which I fought both my churning belly and the desire to grab the bag of cookies—more appetizing by the minute—and flee), my parents went upstairs, leaving only us and our awkwardness.

I leaned against the table, not ready to sit. Sandra finished her milk and pushed crumbs around.

"So, hey," she said. She reached into her blue and white

purse (*when had* Sandra *started carrying a purse?*) and retrieved a green Jolly Rancher. "Want one?"

I shook my head. Inside, I was shouting, *Why are you here?* My mouth didn't want to make words, though, so I stayed quiet.

"I haven't been over in a while," she began. Maybe her mouth didn't want to work either, because she stopped after that.

"No," I managed. "You haven't." Once my lips moved, it was easier to continue. "So why today?"

Sandra shrugged, tilted her head to the ceiling, and fiddled with her napkin. "Just thought I'd come by. See if you wanted to do something." The Jolly Rancher clacked against her teeth. Annoying. How had I listened to that for so long?

What?! Why would I want to do something with you? We haven't spoken in weeks, and the last time we did, you were a total jerk. That's what I thought about saying. What came out was, "Where's Lively?" My voice was rough sandpaper.

For a second, an expression of hurt crossed her face. She crunched the candy and I caught a whiff of fake apple. Then she went back to a neutral expression. "Away this weekend with her dad."

So this is best friends outside of school, I thought. *You hang out with me when Lively isn't around and you have nothing better to do.* The dull ache I'd felt for so long was gone, replaced by a sense of calm. Like Lively, Sandra could only hurt me if I let her.

"So I was thinking maybe we could do something?" She swallowed the last of her Jolly Rancher.

"Can't," I said, not taking her bait. "I promised my cousin Kathleen that I'd help her with her wedding favors this afternoon."

"Tomorrow, then? We could get caramel sundaes and go to Becker Books. I haven't been there in ages."

"Really?" Becker Books was one of Sandra's favorite places.

She shrugged. "Lively likes to hang out at Catch 'N' Kick in the mall. Or at my house." She kept her eyes on the table.

Until she mentioned Lively again, I was tempted. The Old Celeste—the one who had never met Model Celeste or worked on Operation Skinny Celeste—would have said yes right away, would have leaped tall buildings to have a sundae with her former best friend. Even New Celeste felt the urge to go, but New Celeste also hadn't eaten an Oreo or had a sundae or root beer in over a month. New Celeste knew how to deal with temptation.

"Uh-uh. Can't." My heart beat harder.

"Are you busy?" Sandra asked.

"Not really," I said. "I'm just not into that anymore." *Thunk, thunk, thunk* went my heart.

"Sundaes?" Sandra said, confused.

"Those too," I responded. *I can't believe I'm saying this!* A blend of pride and fear spread through me.

"Can I get a clue, please? What else aren't you into besides sundaes?"

I took a breath. "Being friends with someone who wants to hang out with me only when she has no other plans."

Sandra's mouth opened so wide I could see the green stripe the Jolly Rancher left on her tongue. But there was nothing more to say, and she knew it. She closed it, swallowed a few times, and pushed back from the table. I stepped aside as she left the kitchen. The front door banged shut behind her.

That felt better than any sundae or cookie ever tasted, I thought.

Red Bathing Suit Woman cheered.

Chapter 25

LATER THAT AFTERNOON, Mom dropped me off at Kathleen's apartment for Dinner and Decoupaging. The ride came with a price, though: extensive questioning about What Went On in the Kitchen With Sandra. My answers were simple. "We talked. I told her I was busy. She left." That didn't satisfy Mom at all.

"I don't know why you won't tell me the truth," she said. "Something's gone on between the two of you."

"It doesn't matter," I responded, annoyed. "What difference does it make? We talked. She left. That's it."

"I just want to make sure you're not upset," she said. "You've had a tough week."

"I'm fine, Mom, really. Not upset." *A few weeks ago? That's another story*, I added to myself. And it was true. I no longer needed Sandra to stick up for me, or make me feel good about my life. Realizing that was like losing a couple of pounds just from breathing. I felt lighter.

"As long as you're sure." She sighed. "I just wish you'd

reconsider finishing the Modeling Challenge. There's only one more event." Could you get whiplash from a subject change? My stomach squeezed into a ball.

We'd stopped in front of Kathleen's building.

"I don't want to talk about it anymore," I said, focusing on the dashboard in front of me to prevent the tears that filled my eyes from falling. "Please don't ask me again." Then I got out of the car. I closed the door and didn't look back, fighting the newly created anxiety in my belly.

Kathleen buzzed me in. To calm down, I walked up the three flights to her apartment. When I reached the top flight, without thinking about it, I paused to catch my breath. After a second, I realized that I didn't have to. I felt winded, but not nearly as much as I would have a few weeks earlier.

You sure it's still the Negative Twenty? Red Bathing Suit Woman asked. I didn't answer, but my chest puffed with pride.

Down the hall, Kathleen's door opened. "Hey," she called, "what're you doing down there?"

I smiled and waved. When I reached her, she gave me a big hug. That day she was wearing one of Paul's UCLA T-shirts and a pair of jeans, and she still looked like a model. Her hair twisted in a knot at her neck.

"Celeste, you look fantastic," she said, leading me into her living room. I knew she wasn't referring to the wrap shirt I'd changed into while riding my good mood after Sandra left. "What've you been doing the past couple of weeks?"

My face warmed, and I shrugged. "You know, the usual. School . . . stuff like that."

She nodded.

"Are you getting excited for the wedding?" I asked to distract her.

"Can't wait, but we still have lots to do. I'm glad you're here to help." She smiled.

When I stepped into the apartment's small dining room, I could see why. It was Arts and Crafts Central: A plastic sheet covered the table, dozens of boxes of clear votive candle holders piled on top of it. Several packages of multicolored tissue paper, sponge brushes, and a big tub of glue were in the mix as well.

"The votives are going on the dinner tables," Kathleen said. "We're going to cover the holders with tissue paper, so when the candle is lit, they'll glow through the colored paper."

"I'm sure it'll be great," I said, not quite able to picture it.

She caught my hesitation. "I'll show you," she said. "Have a seat."

Kathleen removed sheets of pale pink and yellow tissue paper from one of the packages, then tore them into big pieces. She put a candle holder over two of her fingers, smeared the exterior with decoupage paste, wrapped it in tissue, and spread more paste over it.

"Voila," she said. "The paste dries clear."

"Oh, now I get it. That's really cool. I can do that."

"Great, because I've got seventy-five of them that we need to cover. Let's get to work." She handed me a sponge brush and a candle holder.

After scraping a couple of soggy, over-glued pieces of

tissue off a candle holder, I got the hang of it. We sat on either side of the table, crafting, working in silence until we built a rhythm: smear, stick, smear. The finished holders were returned to the boxes for easy transportation to the reception site.

"So," Kathleen asked after a few minutes, "what's all this I hear about the Modeling Challenge? How's that going?"

"I'm, uh, not doing that anymore," I said, focusing on aligning pieces of pink and yellow tissue instead of Kathleen.

"Oh," she said. "That's too bad. I thought your mom said that it didn't conflict with the wedding."

"It doesn't—didn't. I'm just . . . It just didn't work out," I said. I placed my finished holder in a box and went on to the next one without meeting her eyes.

"Mmm." Kathleen finished hers and began another.

"It wasn't for me," I said to fill the silence.

"Did you hate it?"

I put down my candle holder and considered her question. As much as I didn't want to *be* Miss HuskyPeach, I *didn't* hate the process. Parts of it, like meeting Christian, Violet, and Ashley and Gail, were actually fun. The interview was awful because I *made it* awful by not answering Erika's questions. Nearly squashing her and getting Bra Bombed were accidents. In fact, I had been so intent on not wanting to win that I hadn't let myself enjoy the parts of it I liked.

"No," I said, surprised at my answer. "I didn't hate it." I didn't know what to say next. Now that I realized the truth, I wasn't sure what to do with it.

"When I did Miss Teen," Kathleen said, "lots of people couldn't understand why I liked it. Believe it or not, my *mom* didn't understand why I wanted to do it."

Surprised, I dropped my sponge brush into my lap. "Your mom entered me in the Challenge! I thought that's what she did for you."

"Stay still, I'll get some water for that," Kathleen said, retrieving the brush for me. From the kitchen, she said, "I know; it's crazy. I wanted to do the pageant because I read an article about it in some teen magazine. It sounded glamorous."

She returned with a damp dishcloth. "Mom freaked out about it—like she freaks out about everything—but I talked her into it. And the scholarship money they offered as prizes didn't hurt either."

I dabbed at my track pants, wiping the glue away. "That's what she and my mom were so excited about."

"But not you."

I shook my head. "Not really. Besides, being Miss Teen is a lot more glamorous than being Miss HuskyPeach."

Kathleen picked up her sponge brush and another candle holder. "I guess. It's all about what you want to get out of it, though. For me, it was about wearing fun clothes, learning the makeup tricks, and meeting new people. I made friends doing it."

I've gotten humiliated, I thought. *Several times.*

Humiliation builds character, Red Bathing Suit Woman chimed in. *You've also started wearing fun clothes, learned some makeup tricks—or tried to—and met new people.*

I ignored her.

"But it was never about what I wanted," I said. I ceased crafting. "That's the problem. That's why I was trying—" I cut myself off before I could say anything else.

"Trying to what?" Kathleen asked.

"Nothing." I grabbed my candle holder and spread more glue on it than it needed.

"Trying to quit? To back out?"

I shook my head.

"To lose?"

Her words pinned me to my chair. I shook my head again, but not as quickly as before.

"You were trying to lose the contest," Kathleen said, and laughed. "*That's* what you were doing. Why didn't you just tell your mom and dad that you didn't want to do it?"

I slumped in my seat, half annoyed and half relieved that she figured it out. "I tried to tell Mom, but she was so excited. She really wanted me to go through with it. I know it's silly. You and Kirsten said to just tell her and get it over with, and I couldn't." Tears burned my eyes, turning the tissue paper piles into a kaleidoscope of color.

"You didn't want to disappoint her," she said quietly.

"I didn't want to be a fat model." There. I said it out loud.

"But then you liked parts of the experience," she said, beginning to catch on.

I nodded, miserable.

"And then . . . what? Something happened, right?" She leaned over the table. "Something that made you want to quit even though you were enjoying some of it."

Another nod.

"What was it? Did someone find out who you didn't want to know?"

I shook my head.

"Did one of the judges say something to you?"

I shook my head again.

"Celeste, let's not play Twenty Questions. Out with it. What happened?"

"Fine." I let out a big whoosh of breath, inhaled, and told her. I told her all about blowing the interview, cheesing up the photo shoot, falling on Erika, my loose dress, Violet's quick fix, and the horror of the Top-Dropping Bra Bombing. She decoupaged the whole time I spoke, which made it easier, actually. I didn't have to look in her eyes.

When I finished, she put down her sponge brush. "That was the last straw, huh?"

"A pretty big one," I replied.

It was her turn to nod. "Celeste, you know that you won't win, based on everything that's happened, right?"

"Yeah," I said, not sure what she meant.

"So why not go back for the last time and actually let yourself enjoy what you've liked about it?"

"But everyone saw me," I said. "My *dress* fell down."

"Everyone there was a mom, contestant, or stylist—all people who have what you have, have seen them before, or, in the case of the professionals there, don't care because they see them all the time. And you *weren't* facing the audience when it happened. So even if they saw what you have—big deal. Now go and show them what you've got."

I picked up a candle holder and glued while I let her words sink in. I went through a lot not to win, but, like Kathleen hinted, I'd gotten a lot more out of the HuskyPeach contest than I expected. Ashley and Gail, for one (or two). After seeing how mean Faux-Best Friend Sandra could be, and becoming closer to Millie and Katy, I was ready for new friends who liked me for who I was.

Also, I *had* liked how I looked with Christian's makeup magic, and I knew that the contest helped me stick to Operation Skinny Celeste. Even without Miss HuskyPeach, I still hadn't eaten any junk. While I certainly wasn't skinny, I did feel a heck of a lot better—and, according to more and more people, I *looked* better too. I'd never have Mom's and Aunt Doreen's metabolism, but that was old news. And with Lively leaving me alone, and Sandra out of the picture, New Celeste deserved her chance to make an entrance on her own terms.

Besides, any entrance you make has to be better than your last exit, Red Bathing Suit Woman said.

I hated to admit it, but she had a point.

Kathleen didn't ask me any more questions about the Modeling Challenge, and until we finished the candle holders, the rest of our conversation focused on the wedding. Her words about the HuskyPeach stuck with me the whole time, though.

As I gathered my stuff together to leave—she was dropping me off, then meeting Paul to go over seating arrangements—something occurred to me.

"Kathleen?"

"Mmmm?" she responded, searching her purse for the car keys.

"You said one of the reasons why you did Miss Teen was because you wanted to learn the makeup tricks, but you barely wear any."

"That's what I learned," she said. We stepped into the hall and she locked the door.

"What do you mean?"

"When you wear all that stuff for the pageants, you realize something."

"What's that?"

She smiled. "A little lip gloss goes a long way."

Chapter 26

ALL WEEK I avoided talking with my mother about Miss HuskyPeach. Several times, Mom reminded me that she hadn't called to withdraw my candidacy. "If you change your mind, just let me know," she said. I'd never respond, just go on with whatever I was doing. Besides, as it got closer to Saturday, Mom became more and more preoccupied with helping Aunt Doreen with last-minute wedding stuff. She picked up the Monstrosity the Wednesday before the wedding, and it hung on the back of my door to await its debut.

Thursday morning, as I was getting ready to leave for school, she stopped me.

"Come straight home today, hon," she said. "We need to go to the mall for a few things."

What more could I need? I had the dress and the shoes. Even after six weeks of Operation Skinny Celeste, hitting the mall with mom still did not hold any appeal.

At school I shuffled through my two morning classes, then met up with Millie and Katy in the hall before gym.

"More soccer today," said Millie, rolling her eyes. "Can't wait."

"Hey—maybe Celeste will get another chance to try and bust Lively's bust," Katy responded. As they laughed, my cheeks warmed. I felt bad about aiming for her chest. After it happened, I realized it was something that she would probably do to someone else. And I didn't want to be anything like Lively Carson.

Too bad she actually caught it, Red Bathing Suit Woman snickered, clearly not in agreement with me.

We wove our way through the locker room, and I left them at my row. As I dug through my backpack for my fresh gym clothes, my fingers skidded off slick plastic. *The gift card.* I pulled it out.

After riding around in the depths of my bag for weeks, the card was dusty and scratched. The green cardboard backing, emblazoned in white with "A Catch 'N' Kick Gift For You," was creased. The upper left corner was missing. I smoothed it out as best I could on the bench next to me, then wriggled into my sweats and AlHo T-shirt.

Coach's whistle blew, calling everyone to the shower area. On autopilot, I tossed my backpack and school clothes into my locker, slamming the door when finished. The gift card still sat on the bench.

"Let's go!" Coach's voice echoed off the tile and bounced to my row. With neither pockets nor bag, my only options were to bring the card with me or open the locker to put it away, ensuring that I'd have to run laps for lateness. I grabbed the card and scooted into the shower area just as Coach started taking attendance. Since I was late, I ended up sitting near the front, not in my customary corner with Millie and Katy. They smiled at me from across the room.

"Sandra's not here, so I'm going to switch Joanie from team A to team C and Lively from C to B. You'll both play your same positions," Coach said. I was so close, I could count the stains on her sneakers. *One . . . two . . . three . . .* Sweat slicked the gift card clutched in my hand.

I hadn't even noticed Sandra's absence. Lively started whispering to everyone near her, asking where Sandra was.

"Is there a problem with your reassignment, Ms. Carson?" Coach Anapoli asked . . . *thirteen . . . fourteen . . . fifteen . . .*

"Uh, no Coach," Lively responded. "I was just wondering if Sandra is okay. Where is she?"

Coach shrugged. "Not my business or yours, is it?" As Lively scowled, she sent us down to the fields. I'd counted thirty-seven sneaker spots.

I stood to the side, letting the other girls pass as I waited for Katy and Millie.

"What's that?" Millie asked, pointing at my clenched fist.

"Oh. Uh, nothing," I said. I didn't want to explain about the gift card, or why I hadn't given it to Coach yet. I'd been explaining things to people an awful lot over the past few weeks. This was something I needed to do by myself.

I lagged behind them on the walk, creasing the cardboard backing around the card clenched in my fist, worrying about what I'd say to Coach. Would I have to remind her why I was giving it to her? It'd been so long, I wondered if she would remember.

She'll remember, Red Bathing Suit Woman said. *Even after all these weeks. I guarantee you.*

When we reached the field, I went through warm-ups with my team. Coach told us to start and took her clipboard to the sidelines. Some of the girls kicked the ball around to look like they were playing, but no games would begin for real until Coach yelled at us. This was my chance.

I slipped out of the goal and trudged toward the sidelines. Every step felt as heavy as it had the day of Yurk Fest, and my heart pounded a staccato rhythm. My hands were so sweaty, I imagined the ink on the cardboard staining my palm green. *What if it runs so much she can't read the card?* I thought. Too quickly, I was standing in front of Coach Anapoli. I took a deep breath.

"Uhhh, Coach," I started, mouth as dry as Femur, the thighbone bathroom pass from science class. I cleared my throat. "Umm."

She looked up with wide eyes and scooted down the bench, away from me. "Sick, Harris?"

"No," I said, and shook my head hard. Coach relaxed, then resumed staring at her clipboard. I fiddled with the creased cardboard with both hands, keeping my eyes on the top of Coach's head. I took a deep breath. "It's just that . . . I . . ." The temperature of my cheeks rose. If she were watching me, Coach would be in danger of getting a sunburn.

"Don't want to hear it, then. Just play the game." Her eyes remained glued to the clipboard.

Those words, so similar to the ones she'd used a few weeks before, burned hotter than my cheeks. I went from feeling the heat of shame to the flame of irritation.

"I'm not sick," I said, and crossed my arms. "And I'm not trying to get out of class." That got her attention. She shifted her gaze from the clipboard to me. Jaw tight, eyebrows furrowed, she waited to hear what the next excuse would be. I held my sweaty fist out to her and gulped. "I just wanted to apologize for ruining your shoes." I opened my hand and revealed the slick gift card stuck to its soggy backing. My palm *did* have a distinct green tint to it.

"Oh." Her expression smoothed into one of surprise. "Thank you, Celeste." She reached for the gift card, and although a flicker of distaste at its damp texture crossed her face, her wide smile more than made up for it. A weight that I wasn't even aware I'd been carrying disappeared.

I smiled back. "You're welcome."

"And good work filling out those food logs. You're the only one who did them consistently, and turned in the extra-credit ones. It shows."

My smile stretched even wider. "Thanks."

"Now get to your game. Girls!" she shouted around me. "I'd better see some soccer soon, otherwise you'll be running laps."

Heart slowing, hands drying, I crossed the field, back to my team.

And one thing I noticed? Coach's infamous tracksuit hadn't smelled bad at all.

Chapter 27

AFTER WE FINISHED our game, I met Millie and Katy on the walk back to the locker room. They wanted to know what I'd been talking to Coach Anapoli about, but I shrugged them off. As I was changing the subject, there was a sharp poke in my back.

"Hey," Lively said, appearing at my side. "Where's Sandra?"

"How should we know," Katy replied. "You're the one who's glued to her all the time."

Lively narrowed her eyes. Her ant-friends gathered behind her, eager to hear whatever taunts she'd fling. "I wasn't *talking* to you," she said through gritted teeth. "I'd never talk to you."

"You just did," Millie said, smirking. She turned to me. "Don't you think Lively is looking a little . . . uneven today?"

Confusion dotted Lively's friends' expressions—and mine too, I'm sure. But I caught on fast. I gave Katy and Millie a huge grin.

"Absolutely."

A flash of panic crossed Lively's face, then she was back to her Mask of Superiority. She had probably decided that ignoring the comments was the best way to deal with the situation. She directed her question back to me. "Well, where is she?"

"Dunno," I said. "I told her I didn't want to hang out with her anymore." At this point, we had arrived at the locker room. Millie and Katy, probably surprised at my announcement, stopped short just inside the doorway and gave me identical wide-eyed expressions. Lively, seeing that we didn't have the information she needed, flounced past us to change before the bell. As she did, I heard her mutter something to one of her ant-friends about going to Sandra's house for dinner, and how Sandra *had* to be okay because she thought "he was getting off work early" and would be there.

That was when everything made sense. Lively's sudden interest in Sandra . . . the comments that Kirsten had been making . . . Sandra's complaint about where Lively liked to hang out in the mall . . . Lively had a crush on Sandra's brother Geoff! The realization hit me in a wave, causing me to stop halfway to my locker. I shook my head. *Wait 'til Millie and Katy hear this,* I thought. Unlike my Secret Gift Card Delivery, *that* was something worth explaining.

Until I got home, I'd forgotten that Mom wanted me to go to the mall with her. She was ready as soon as I got in the door, keys in hand, barely letting me put my bag down before ushering me to the car.

"I promised your aunt that I'd be back in time to help her finish the seating chart," she explained, hustling me more effectively than Coach Anapoli ever had. *Had she taken lessons from Christian?* I thought as we sped away. I still wasn't clear on what we needed.

Once we arrived at the mall, though, it was obvious. She ushered me straight to The Lace Slipper, the "unmentionables" store on the second level.

"Mom!" I said as we entered.

"I want to make sure you have a strapless bra that fits you properly," she explained. "You need it for your bridesmaid dress." I rolled my eyes.

I needed it two weeks ago at the HuskyPeach, I wanted to reply. Instead, I stayed quiet. Why make this any worse than it had to be?

It got worse.

The grandmotherly saleslady was very "hands-on," insisting on coming into the dressing room with me with an armful of underwire, elastic, and lace. "See?" she said, spinning me to face the hated mirror. "This one doesn't have large enough cups. You're overflowing." I nodded my head, avoiding my reflection. *Even Violet sticking her hands down my top wasn't this awkward.*

It took five bras to find the one that made the saleslady happy. She praised the boning and the "uplift," while I praised the end of the ordeal. Mom took the purchase to the cash register and I fled to the front of the store.

"That wasn't so bad, was it?" Mom asked on our way out. I shot her my Annoyed Look, but she wasn't paying attention. "I also thought we might want to pick out some new clothes for you, as another reward for the positive changes you've made recently."

Inside, I groaned. *Oh, come on,* Red Bathing Suit Woman chided. *It's not going to be like it usually is—promise.*

You'd better be right. I exhaled. "Fine. Let's get a few things."

We went into the HuskyPeach, where a big sign outside the door advertised the San Francisco fashion show.

"I just wish you'd reconsider." She sighed, then stopped, examining the sign with a sad expression.

"No way," I said, tugging her arm to get her moving. What little shopping enthusiasm I'd mustered drooped.

Mom cruised the racks, pulling out several jewel-toned shirts and a couple of pairs of pants. This time, most of the stuff I tried on fit me better, and we even agreed on three shirts and one pair of pants. At the cash register, Mom took the bag from the saleslady like she was receiving a trophy. I guess, in a way, we both were.

Before we reached the mall exit closest to our car, she stopped again, this time in front of the Catch 'N' Kick.

"I need to run in here for one second. Ben needs a wrap for his elbow before his next game."

"Mom—" I protested, but she was already inside. I sighed, then followed.

The big bin of tennis balls was still in the middle of the

store. I parked myself there, watching Mom approach Geoff at the counter, humming along to the mall-music version of "Dreaming Without You." Geoff waved at me and flashed a big smile. I smiled and waved back. *It's easy to see why Lively has a crush on him,* I thought. *Why anyone would.*

As I finished the thought, I heard the chatty, giggling commotion that signaled the arrival of a certain group of girls. When I turned, the Blond Ponytail Brigade was bopping into the store. They huddled at the front, around the baseball jerseys. I turned away. Geoff was leading Mom in my direction.

"They're right over here," he said, "in the tennis section." After he pointed her to the appropriate display, he faced me. "Hey Celeste," he said.

"Hey," I responded, staring at my shoes. Behind me, the giggling got louder. I peeked up at Geoff. He stared over my head, eyes narrowed. He blinked down to me. Silence. Not a giggle to be heard.

"Haven't seen you at the house lately," he said. I shrugged, watching the floor, playing with the tie on my wrap shirt. "Everything okay?"

I nodded. He put his hand on my shoulder and bent down close to me. Inside, my belly wiggled. "You look really good, Celeste. Keep it up." Then he straightened.

Between the warmth of his hand and his words, I thought I would explode from pride and embarrassment. But the tingly feeling didn't last long.

I felt the eyes on me like hot coals before I turned around. Lively stood on the far side of a rack of tennis dresses.

"Hi, Geoff?" she purred, drawing her blond ponytail over one shoulder.

Bet she's seen that in a movie, Red Bathing Suit Woman said.

"Sandra, um, she wasn't in school today, so I was wondering if she's okay?"

"Did you call her?" he asked. His voice sounded detached, like he didn't want to talk, but was out of politeness. He didn't look at her.

"Uh, well, I was going to," Lively said, ignoring my presence, "but I didn't want to disturb her if she was actually, you know, sick. So I thought I'd ask you." She stepped closer to him. Geoff backed up.

She didn't wait for him to respond. "I had something else to ask you," she said. Her attention flickered in my direction. "But it's private."

"I'm working," Geoff said, his voice gruff. I saw his shoulders stiffen under his green Catch 'N' Kick shirt.

Lively put on a huge, sunny fake smile. "I know. But it's important. I thought, maybe, one day, we could—"

"Honey," Mom said to me, interrupting Lively, elbow wrap in her hand, "I've got it. Let's go." She moved in the direction of the cash register.

"Bye, Mrs. Harris," Geoff said. "We could what?" he directed at Lively. Exasperation wafted from him in a cloud.

Lively shifted from foot to foot, clearly flustered. Half of me wanted to witness her next move, but the other half knew I'd seen enough already—more than she wanted me to, that's for sure.

I stepped away from the tennis ball bin but didn't get very far. The tie on my wrap shirt had somehow twisted around the metal cage when I was playing with it. Not wanting to draw attention to myself, I tried to subtly untangle it. No dice. Plus, I was still between Geoff and Lively. And I guess she decided that she had to go through with her plan, whether or not I watched.

"Umm, go . . ." she began, trying to find the words.

I busied myself with my predicament, this time giving the shirt a firmer tug.

"Celeste, do you need help with that?" Geoff said. He sounded relieved to have something to do. He came closer.

"Out. Somewhere. Or hang out," Lively blurted.

She did not *just do that!*

Before I could process my shock, Lively took a step in my direction. Her expression switched back and forth from fear to fury. Geoff's attention was solely on me. My face burned. Although no longer afraid of Lively, I certainly didn't need to hand her ammunition.

"Oh, I get it," Geoff said, like he hadn't even heard her, studying the bin as though it was the most interesting piece of store equipment he'd ever seen. "You've gotten wrapped around the gate." His hand slid between the bin and me, and a thrill shot through me at being so close to him. "I'm just going to slide this open and you'll be all set. A couple of the tennis balls might slip out, so be careful."

Lively's glare, which I could see over Geoff's head, would have turned Medusa to stone. I heard the click of a latch, then my shirt pulled tight, and all at once I was free.

Geoff must not have secured the gate properly, however, because as I stepped away an avalanche of green tennis balls bounced from the bin.

"Whoa!" Geoff said, trying to close the gate. "Be careful." He latched it, stopping the Green Tide, but tennis balls rolled every which way around the floor. Lively mouthed *cow* at me while his back was turned.

"Sorry," I mumbled, feeling responsible.

"Not your fault," Geoff said. "I'll just scoop these up; it's no problem." He smiled again.

Did he let them loose to avoid dealing with Little Miss Ponytail Stalker? Red Bathing Suit Woman whispered.

Think so, was my response.

"I'll help!" Lively called, probably wanting another shot at asking Geoff out. Her gaggle of girls, which had slipped farther into the store, nodded in agreement. They scrambled for tennis balls.

"Really, it's not—" Geoff began, but he was too late. It was a neon green Easter egg hunt—the girls weaved through racks and peeked under displays to find the balls. I just wanted to get to my mom at the cash register and get out of there.

"It's no problem," Lively said, struggling to keep her eyes on Geoff while she picked up tennis balls. "I like helping out." She backed up, scooping them into her arms, not paying attention where she was going.

It happened the same way it would in a movie.

Like in slow motion, I saw her foot land squarely on a tennis ball and the shock flash across her face as she realized she was losing balance. Her arms flailed, releasing the five or six balls she'd gathered, sending them bouncing in front of her. She clutched the nearest clothing rack. I thought she regained her balance, but instead it just changed her direction. She fell facedown, right on top of some of the renegade balls.

"Are you okay?" Geoff said. He rushed to her side.

"I—I think so." Lively sniffed, her cheeks scarlet.

Geoff held out a hand to help her up, which she gratefully took. Glad, I was sure, to be rescued by her Knight in Green Catch 'N' Kick Uniform.

As she stood, she revealed the full extent of the damage. Smack in the middle of Lively's now-flat chest were two big wet spots. Geoff's eyes were immediately drawn to them, as were mine and those belonging to the crowd of ant-friends and other shoppers who had gathered as witnesses to Lively's fall. The Red Bathing Suit Woman cackled.

Realization did not come swiftly.

"What? I'm okay," Lively said. She smoothed her hair and went to straighten her shirt.

"Did you drop a bottle of water?" I asked. I couldn't help myself.

Then she knew. She crossed her arms tight over her chest.

"Honey, do you need a tissue?" my mom asked, digging through her purse. Next to us, Geoff gawked.

If she hadn't called me "cow" and "spew," if she hadn't stolen my best friend simply because she liked his brother, if she hadn't said terrible things to me every time I made a mistake . . . if she hadn't done all those things, I would have felt bad for her. Really bad.

But she had.

So when she burst into tears and ran out of the store, leaving behind a herd of shell-shocked girls and a very confused Geoff—and I smiled, I felt pretty okay about it.

Chapter 28

LIVELY DIDN'T COME to school on Friday, but that didn't stop the rumors—Lively stuffed her bra, her implants exploded, someone threw a water balloon at her (I think one of her ant-friends started that one, to try and save Lively from embarrassment. Not that it worked) . . . Sandra suffered a little too. Seemed that everyone except Sandra had known why Lively wanted to be friends with her. She slunk around school, ashamed about the whole thing.

After social studies, she appeared beside my locker. I twisted the combination into the dial without meeting her gaze, not sure if I was supposed to do the talking.

"Did you know?" she asked, using a soft voice.

I considered my answer while switching the books in my backpack.

"I figured it out," I said. Then I added, "It was pretty obvious," because, although I didn't have any desire to be mean to Sandra since that day in the kitchen, I didn't want her to think I was friendly. On one hand, I felt bad for

Sandra because everyone knew she'd been used, but on the other, she'd treated me so poorly that I wasn't going to jump up and down and be her friend again.

"I was stupid," she said.

"Mmm-hmmm." New Celeste was no dishrag. Sandra needed to say the words herself; I wasn't about to give them to her. I zipped my backpack and closed the locker. The warning bell rang.

"And mean," she finished. "I'm sorry." Millie emerged from the crowd of students moving to their next class. She stood behind Sandra but didn't say anything.

"Thanks," I said. "You were mean." We stood in silence.

"You've been working really hard," she said. She wasn't talking about my attempts at friendship.

I nodded. "I have."

"It shows. Your outfit is cute," she said, shy. It was a green shirt and black flowy pants combo from my recent mall visit with mom. She still wore the Lively Special.

Who needs a new "look" now? Red Bathing Suit Woman snickered, in a *Lord of the Flies* type of mean way. I didn't acknowledge either of them.

"Are we still . . . Can we hang out sometime?" Sandra tried. Her eyes were big and sad and hopeful, all at the same time, like a puppy begging for attention. My insides twisted, seeing that expression on her face—*one that she'd probably seen on me several times over the past few weeks,* I reminded myself. I sighed. Honesty is definitely the best policy in these situations.

"I don't know," I replied. So much stuff had happened

and changed—and *I* had changed—that I didn't know what our friendship would be like anymore.

She nodded like she understood, then slipped into the crowd to go to her next class, barely glancing at Millie as she passed.

"About time she apologized," Millie said at my side. We started our walk to science. I shrugged.

"Hey, Celeste," Alan Okuri, Mike's friend, stopped us. "Did you really see Lively's explosion?"

I was surprised. Alan barely said two words to me in the years we'd been at AlHo. *But he's been paying you a lot more attention recently,* Red Bathing Suit Woman pointed out. What did that mean?

Millie gave me a nudge. "Uh . . . explosion? It was more like . . . deflation," I finished. He laughed, showing dimples.

"Can, uhh . . . you tell me about it sometime?" he asked, with a nervous squeak to his voice.

My face flamed. "Sure, I guess," I answered.

"Cool." He walked with us in silence. We reached the science room door. "Your shirt's a nice color," he said, and went to his seat. The back of his neck glowed red.

"You're quite the celebrity now," Millie said as we took our own seats. "Looks like you've even got an admirer."

"People will forget about it by Monday." *Did she really think Alan liked me? Did I want him to? He was nice . . . and smart . . .*

"Doubt it," she said, gesturing at our classmates. "They

can't wait for her to show up." Someone made the lab water fountain squirt.

Maybe they wouldn't forget after all.

I had to forget about Lively and the water bra for a while, though, thanks to the wedding rehearsal that night. Kathleen glowed with happiness and even Aunt Doreen enjoyed herself at the dinner after. As we said good night, I found myself in a conversation with Aunt Doreen, Mom, and Kathleen.

"What time do you have to be in San Francisco tomorrow?" Aunt Doreen asked, turning to me.

"Nine o'clock," I said, before Mom could respond. "We have to get up early."

Mom's Questioning Eyebrows were outmatched by her Open Mouth of Shock.

"Yes, very early," she said, when her mouth started working again. Behind her, Kathleen winked at me.

On our way to the car, Mom asked what had happened. I told her I changed my mind. I think she was afraid that I'd change it back, because she didn't ask again and just smiled all the way home.

The truth was, I'd done a lot of thinking over the past two weeks. Between Kathleen's conversation during our decoupage session, and Millie's and Katy's encouragement, I realized that the pageant *had* been good for me. I lost *some* weight over its six weeks—about nine pounds of the Negative Twenty—which wasn't a bad start (I'd caved in and finally approached the scale). Plus, I felt better about myself. As Sandra noticed, I'd been wearing fewer hoodies and track pants, and Wrap Shirt Tennis Tangle or not, I liked how I felt in different types of clothes. The final round of the HuskyPeach, I decided, would be the way for me to do the pageant because I wanted to—not because Mom or Aunt Doreen or anyone else wanted me to be there.

I woke up the next morning expecting to feel nervous. Instead, it was excitement that made my hands tingle. I reminded myself of what Kathleen said: Let yourself enjoy the parts you like. For the first time since the beginning of the whole Husky Fiasco, I showered and dressed in a flash. Since I needed to be at the Embarcadero Center early to get ready, Mom took me. Dad and Ben would come up later.

The nuttiness at the PeachWear warehouse was nothing compared to the barely controlled chaos of the Embarcadero. The mall was transformed into a stage and runway—the exact one from round two. I flashed back to the Top-Dropping Bra Bombing, then pushed the thought away. Signs directed the stylists and contestants to various check-in locations, but most moms and girls were ignoring them, wandering around the stage taking pictures instead. The ever-present Guides in Black tried to keep order and encouraged people to sign in.

At *least there are no boxes on conveyor belts overhead*, I thought.

"This is so exciting," Mom said, squeezing my shoulder. For once, I agreed.

I gasped as we emerged from the shopping area into the center rotunda. Giant photos of each contestant hung on every other column surrounding the stage.

"They must be from round one," I murmured, examining a bedsheet-sized portrait of Gail, done in black and white. Her dark hair feathered over one shoulder and her dramatic almond-shaped eyes stared out at us. The effect was breathtaking.

"We should find yours," Mom said. Now I understood why the other moms and contestants were milling around.

I was about to agree when I remembered what I'd done during my shoot. "Uh, Mom, I don't know if we should search for it right now," I said. Grinning like a cartoon character probably wouldn't translate well to six thousand times normal size. Mom would have none of it, though. She tugged me around like I was Couscous on a leash, gawking at each photo. Ashley's was just as stunning as Gail's. Her smile was as wide as the Golden Gate Bridge and her eyes sparkled. After hers, there was only one picture-column left.

I dragged my feet, but there was no avoiding the inevitable. When we reached the front of the column, I nearly laughed out loud in relief.

The girl in the photo stared straight at the camera, over one shoulder, in a tight close-up. She had dark hair, waved around her face. Her round eyes were so big and black you could see the reflection of the spotlights in them. Her skin was as smooth as marble, and her lips pursed in a pout. Developing it in black and white made every shadow and line on her face more dramatic.

My *picture was so bad that they used one of some other girl!*
The only problem was, I couldn't figure out who.

"Honey," Mom whispered.

"I'm sorry, Mom," I said. I couldn't think of anything else
to say. *She must be furious.*

"Sorry?" she said, turning her gaze to me. "Honey, you
are beautiful. Don't you see?"

"Mom, that's not—"

But it was. When Mom said it, I saw it.

Shadow Nate had picked one of my few serious shots. It
was better than any school picture I'd ever take in my life.
Mom was right—it *was* me, in a way I'd never seen myself
before. Model Celeste looked grown-up, serious . . . dare I
say it? Sexy.

Oh yeah! Red Bathing Suit Woman said. I agreed.

Unfortunately, we were interrupted from admiring the
picture any more.

"Hi, Celeste—did I get that right?" Violet Page Explainer
Mom said. She'd emerged from behind my column. Bay-be
smiled at me from her customary spot behind her mother.

"Yes," Mom replied. "So nice to see you."

"So nice to see *you* after that nasty fall you took last time.
That box nearly hit Bay-be," VPE Mom said. Then she said to
Mom, "We didn't think you'd bring her back." Her nameless
daughter watched the floor.

"I didn't *bring* her anywhere," Mom said with pride.
"Celeste *chose* to come today."

"Well," VPE Mom said, clutching her purse close to her
side, and leveling her gaze at me. "How *brave* of you."

"We're going to sign in," Mom said, putting an end to the conversation. "Good luck today," she directed to Bay-be.

"Can you imagine?" Mom said once we moved out of their range. "She thought I would actually force you to do this, like she forces her daughter. I would never put pressure on you like that. I mean—" She stopped.

I stood and waited, contestants and moms milling around me.

"Oh, that's terrible," she said, in a voice so low I wondered if she was speaking to herself or me. "I'm a little dense, I think. You told me that this wasn't what you wanted, and I never listened, did I?" Her eyes filled with tears.

Even though I hated to see her upset, I shrugged. What was there to say?

"Let's go," she said. "We don't need to be here." She turned and walked in the direction we'd just come from.

Finally she gets it, I thought. But leaving wasn't what I wanted now.

"Mom!" I called, trailing after her. "Mom! Wait!" She slowed and let me catch up.

"I'm so sorry, sweetheart," she said. "Let's go. We can go to Aunt Doreen's and get ready for the wedding there."

"I want to be here today, Mom. I *chose* to come back, remember? I might not have wanted this when we got started, but I do now. Let's check in." Other moms and daughters bumped their way around us.

She wrapped me in a big hug. I smelled her fruity shampoo. "You don't have to do this, Celeste. We can go."

"Really, Mom. I want this. Honest." She studied me for a

minute, hands on my shoulders, then squeezed me again.

"You've made a lot of big changes lately, haven't you?" she asked. A blend of warmth and pride spread through me.

"Yeah, I have."

We found our check-in station and were instructed to go to the HuskyPeach boutique on the second level. Frazzled Guide waited at the door. This time, her hair was pulled back in a low knot. *Easier to manage,* I thought. Based on its high shine, it was also shellacked in place with hairspray. Better hairstyle or not, an aura of overwhelming stress surrounded her.

"Moms need to wait in the audience today," she said. "We don't have enough room up here for everyone. You"—she pointed to me—"have to pick up your gown from Elsa before going to hair and makeup. She's in the back of the store." She shooed me in the right direction, but not before I said bye to Mom.

"I'm so proud of you," she responded.

"I'm proud of me too." I smiled.

Upstairs, giant clothing racks framed Elsa, but they looked less out of place in an actual store than in the warehouse. When I reached her, she was instructing Gail how to tie the sash on her electric blue dress. Gail waved at me and Elsa declared her ready to go to hair and makeup.

"You came back!" Gail said, giving me a hug. My heart lifted. "I'm so glad you did. Are you okay?" I nodded.

"I'm fine. And, I got a strapless bra." I gestured with the Lace Slipper bag. Gail grinned. Returning was the right choice.

"To hair and makeup with you," Elsa said again. Gail said bye and scurried away.

"Contestant eleven," I said when Elsa turned her attention to me.

"You were the one with the wrong-sized dress last time," she said. "I felt terrible. I guess the measurements on your card were wrong."

That's because Aunt Doreen guessed when she sent them in, I thought. I put on my Innocent Expression. "What do we do?" I asked.

"I pulled a few items out for you based on what I remembered from your shape last time. Try these on." She gestured to three dresses hanging from a hook on the end of a rack. "If none of them fit, we'll go from there."

I hoisted the three dresses and Elsa directed me to a real changing room. I checked: All three had thick, tank top style straps. Relieved, I tried the first on—a yellow puffy one—and came out.

"It's your size, but not your color," Elsa said. I didn't think it was either. I felt like a taxi. "Try the red one."

I'd like that dress, Red Bathing Suit Woman said. *Matches my outfit.*

Too bad, I replied. *This is for my shape, not yours.*

It was a simple design: long, bell-shaped skirt, a scoop neck, and tank straps. When I put it on, it fit. *No need for the Strapless Wonder,* I thought, relieved.

'Cause the blue floral is so classy under that dress, Red Bathing Suit Woman added.

"Fine," I muttered. As much as I hated the purchasing

process of the Strapless Wonder, it did fit well. And the red dress looked even better on me once I put it on.

"Perfect," Elsa said when I emerged from the dressing room. "You don't need anything else. Leave your clothes in a bag back here, then off to hair and makeup. You're with Christian. He's"—she checked her sheet—"in the accessories department in the front left corner of the store."

I hitched the sides of my skirt and followed her directions. As I approached the shoes, crying and shouting overpowered the store chatter. When I turned the corner, VPE Mom and Frazzled Guide were blocking the aisle.

Aren't moms supposed to be in the audience? I thought. *Typical.*

"My bay-be needs him," VPE Mom wailed. "How could you let this happen! It's the most irresponsible act. I demand that the judges be made aware of this." She pointed her finger at Frazzled Guide, who, in spite of the hairspray, was unraveling.

"All of the judges are aware of the situation," Frazzled Guide soothed. "We've made other arrangements with Sascha downstairs. Christian just wanted to be able to tell all of his clients personally."

"I'm terribly sorry," came Christian's voice from the other side of VPE Mom. "I really do wish I could help out. But Sascha's great. Your daughter is going to love her."

VPE Mom sniffed and complained, but allowed Frazzled Guide to take her arm and escort her downstairs.

They squeezed past me, followed by Bay-be, eyes to the

floor. That revealed the cause of the fuss: Christian's right arm was in a sling.

My Makeup Magician was cursed. And so was I. I instantly developed a new appreciation for VPE Mom's hysterics. My Husky Luck hadn't changed after all.

"You look fabulous," he said, sweeping me into a one-armed hug.

"What happened?" I asked, fighting the edge of panic creeping into my voice.

"Skidded on a damp towel in the salon," he said. "Separated my shoulder."

I winced.

"They assigned everyone a new stylist except you." He held up his good hand when he saw my Face of Panic. "I told them not to."

"You told them *what?*" *Great. Christian thinks it's not worth it for me to compete.* My heart slid to my shoes.

"You don't need Sascha," he said. "You can do this yourself. I promised I'd show you how, right?"

"Doing my own makeup before a huge San Francisco fashion show was not how I thought I'd learn," I responded, this time fighting Hysterical Aunt Doreen Voice.

Even with the sling, Christian's magic was powerful. While we talked, he maneuvered me into his chair, opened his bag, and removed his hand mirror.

"Yet here we are. Are you up for it, or not?" He waited, a mischievous grin on his face, while I considered his offer. Aunt Doreen Hysterics retreated.

Why not? I reasoned. *New Celeste has dealt with harder stuff than this.*

Red Bathing Suit Woman said, *Who knows? For her next trick, maybe she'll let me borrow that dress.*

Not likely, I responded.

"Let's do it," I said, giving Christian my own devious smile.

This time, I swiped, lined, glossed, and shadowed under his direction. He pointed out which brush, wands, and colors to use, and I followed orders. It was like paint by numbers, only on my face.

"Done," he declared, after I'd applied my second coat of mascara. "See? It's easy."

"Easy with you telling me how to do it," I said. I slid off the chair and gave him a half hug. "Think I'll just stick to lip gloss at home, though."

"A little bit goes a long way," he said. I blinked at him. "Rock that room, Celeste."

Chapter 29

FRAZZLED GUIDE PACED at the front of the store, tucking loose hairs from her knot behind her ears. "Good. You're here. Who did your makeup? Never mind. It's time to get in line." She hustled me out the door and downstairs to the sectioned-off backstage area.

"You're behind Ashley. Same as last time; do you remember?" I nodded. The hair came loose again. "Okay, wait here. We start in ten minutes."

"Who *did* do your makeup?" Gail asked. Ashley also seemed interested in my response.

"I did," I answered. A flower of pride bloomed in my chest.

"Wow," said Ashley. "Good for you!"

"Really? I could never do that," Gail said.

"Of course you could," Ashley responded. "Not that you don't look great, Celeste," she added in a hurry, "but . . ." And she went on, boosting Gail's self-confidence.

Erika came by, off her crutches. "Do a head count," she

directed Frazzled Guide, who stood behind me. She waved at me. "I'm better. You?" she mouthed.

"Okay," I mouthed back.

"And gutsy," she added. I grinned. She grinned too, and moved on.

"Head count, head count," Frazzled muttered. "Gail-Ashley-Celeste—where's Rosalie? Have any of you seen Rosalie?" I shook my head along with the other girls.

"Who's Rosalie?" Gail whispered to Ashley and me. Neither of us had any idea.

"None of you move," Frazzled Guide said. "I'll be right back." She spun, and there was a sharp tug at my waist. Then a tearing sound.

It was like someone poured snow down my back.

Not the dress, Red Bathing Suit Woman said. *Tell me it's not the dress.*

"Tell me it's not bad, tell me it's not bad," I said to Ashley. I turned to show her my back, and caught a glimpse of sandy-colored boy hair beyond the backstage ropes as I did so.

She gasped. "Oh no. It must have been her heel." I twisted and tugged on the skirt. The gaping hole where it met the bodice was as big as Couscous—too big to hide or fix in less than ten minutes.

I am never doing this again, I thought.

"Celeste!" called a familiar voice. "Hey! Celeste!" Ben. He squirmed under the velvet ropes into the backstage area.

Don't have time for you right now.

"What're you going to do?" Gail said, shocked. "There's no time."

"Find help," I said. I hitched up my skirt and stepped out of line. Ben followed. "Where's Elsa?" I asked the first guide I saw.

"Audience," she said. Then she saw Ben, and scowled. "No one allowed backstage," she said. Another contestant caught her attention and she strode away.

"Hey Ben," I said, searching for help over his head.

"You look great," he said. His words did it. Tears filled my eyes.

"What's wrong?"

I showed him the hole. "I'm trying to find someone to help me fix it or something else to wear, but I only have a couple of minutes and I don't think that's going to happen." I sniffed, struggling against the tears and not wanting to ruin my makeup. "If I can't fix it, I can't do the show."

Ben looked worried. Then he brightened. "Don't cry, Celeste, I'll get you another one. I know right where it is!"

Not knowing what he was talking about, I nodded and patted him on the head, still scanning the crowd for help. A second later, he disappeared.

The seconds crawled. Around me, contestants stood in line, wearing everything from ball gowns to basics. Guides wove in between the girls, fixing, straightening, smoothing, and counting. Familiar dance music pounded through the mall speakers. I did my best to keep my back to the ropes, pacing and trying to flag down anyone who could help. Heck, I'd even be glad to see Violet's double-stick tape roll . . .

Why are you doing this? Red Bathing Suit Woman asked me. *You don't have anything more to prove. You came back, saw*

Christian, did your makeup. That's it. You don't have to go out there. Show them the torn dress and it's done.

I'm not going to quit, I answered. *I'm going to go through with it no matter what happens, what I have to wear, or who falls over. Stop nagging me before I change my mind.*

"Whose is that?" came a guide's voice from behind me. I spun.

"Pssst! Celeste!" A tug at my saggy skirt.

"Ben!" He was panting hard, holding the plastic-wrapped Monstrosity high above his head. *Of course! The Monstrosity!* Peach lace never looked so good. The hem dragged on the floor, but I didn't care. "Thanks," I said, hugged him, and took the hanger.

"I ran the whole way to the car. And I didn't even hurt myself!"

"You rock star!" I cheered. We high-fived. He scuttled to the audience, beaming.

Where am I going to change? I thought. There was no way I'd have time to get upstairs to the HuskyPeach, and most of the backstage area was exposed. I held the Monstrosity high and worked my way back to my line. When they saw me, Gail and Ashley waved like they were guiding a plane to its airport gate.

"Where'd you get a new dress?" Ashley hissed.

"Two minutes, everybody. Set, please," Erika said as she navigated the crowd. "Two minutes."

There was no place for me to change. In front of us, just above eye level, was the stage. Behind me was open floor and lots of contestants.

"Can you stand in front of me?" I asked Ashley and Gail. Other girls, in lines next to us, heard. Primped heads turned in our direction.

"What are you doing?" Gail said, but she did what she was told. Ashley too.

"Changing," I said. No time for fancy locker room maneuvers. I pulled the plastic off the Monstrosity and hung it on the rear edge of the stage. With a tug, I unzipped the side of the red dress, stepped out of it, and stuffed it underneath the platform. Exposed, I shivered. *Please no one see me, please no one see me,* I begged in my head. Gail and Ashley provided a fairly good screen. I squirmed into the Monstrosity. When I poked my head out, I saw girls from the line to our right gaping.

"Never seen anyone change before?" I snapped. They turned away in a hurry.

Glad you're wearing the Strapless Wonder now, aren't you? Red Bathing Suit Woman said. *You can thank me later.* I rolled my eyes.

"Okay, done," I said to Gail and Ashley. They smoothed my hair, helped me straighten the Monstrosity, and we were back in line like nothing ever happened. "Thanks for being my human screen."

"You're welcome," Ashley said, staring at the lace, mesmerized by the Monstrosity.

"Wow," Gail said. "That's, urm, quite a dress you got there." Before I could respond, the PA system clicked on.

"Ladies and gentlemen," came a familiar voice from the stage. "Welcome to PeachWear Industries' Northern

California Regional Modeling Challenge. I'm Violet Page, and I'll be hosting this morning's event." She explained that the contestants would walk the runway, turn, and wait offstage for the Challenge winner to be announced after the judges finished scoring. As she spoke, the excitement level backstage climbed as fast as the Embarcadero's express elevator. The lights dimmed.

I exchanged nervous smiles with Gail, Ashley, and the girls around us. *Almost done,* I thought.

The first group of girls was called to get ready. A ripple of anticipation spread through me. *No falling boxes this time,* I thought. *And a dress that fits.*

Angelique did a great job with the Monstrosity. Although I couldn't see myself in it, it felt like it was made for me. (It *was,* Red Bathing Suit Woman reminded me.) The seams didn't pull or pinch, the sleeves were comfortable, and no pins stuck out from the bottom. But I'm sure I still looked like a lace-covered refugee from an evil pastel garden party.

Frazzled Guide escorted the second group to the stage. Each time she passed me, the sight of the Monstrosity unglued her even more—her hair frizzed and clumped out of the knot in a halo of stress. The dress horrified her, and she certainly knew it wasn't HuskyPeach-wear, but there was too much going on for her to ask me about it. The first bunch of girls, finished, stood to the side with huge, relieved smiles on their faces. We were the third group. Frazzled Guide gave us her best Get Ready or Else look as the contestants from group two came backstage one at a time. And then they were done.

"You're up," she hissed. "What are you *wearing?*"

"Do you like it?" I asked, and stifled a giggle.

Gail calmly led us to the edge of the stage. This time, she was prepared. She climbed the stairs and did her walk and spin much slower than round two. *Must've practiced,* I thought. *Good for her.* She finished her spin and Ashley went out. I couldn't tell if she chewed her nails.

"Good job," I whispered to Gail when she came down the stairs.

"Go!" Frazzled Guide gave me a push to get moving.

I hitched the sides of the Monstrosity and climbed the steps to the stage. As I went up each one, the beam from the spotlight grew stronger. When I reached the top, I dropped the sides of the skirt and stepped out.

"Our next contestant is wearing—" Violet began. I kept going, passing Ashley and heading straight for the end of the runway. Cheers of "Yeah Celeste" reached me, but because of the lights, it was impossible to see more then a few feet from the edge of the stage. My cheering section remained anonymous, but I was sure I heard Ben.

Owe him a cheer of my own later, I thought.

"Wearing a lovely peach formal gown with delicate lace overlay," Violet recovered. I completed my spin, sent a huge smile in the direction of the judges, and started my walk back.

VPE Mom's daughter passed me. *Right about now is when that box fell,* I thought. But this time there were no Bra Bombs, and I made it offstage with my head held high.

Chapter 30

WHILE THE LAST contestants finished their walks, Ashley, Gail, and some of the other girls whispered and fretted over who would win. I stayed to the side, listening, but caring only that I'd finished. *Miss HuskyPeach can have her crown*, I thought, *and her scholarship money.* Surviving the HuskyPeach Modeling Challenge was prize enough for me.

Cheers and applause signaled the end of the fashion show. The lights brightened.

"All of our models were fantastic today," Violet said. "Let's give them another round of applause." The audience obeyed.

When the noise died down, Violet picked up. "It's been a fun few weeks, and before we crown Miss HuskyPeach, we'd like to ask all the contestants to return to the stage for something very special."

The guides flitted from group to group, putting us in order and hissing instructions in our ears. I filed out with the rest of my line and stood across the back of the stage. The spotlights were blinding. When all the girls were onstage, Violet continued.

"We have a secret guest with us here today who's been patiently sitting out of sight and watching the fashion show on a monitor. Here to perform two of his smash hits, 'Last Night' and 'Dreaming Without You,' please welcome singer/songwriter Theo Christmas!"

"She did NOT just say that," squealed Ashley in my ear over the explosive applause.

"She did! She did!" said Gail. She jumped up and down.

I can't believe I almost didn't come, I thought. My heart was in danger of exploding at the thought of being in the same *room* as Theo Christmas, let alone on the same *stage. I might die. But under the circumstances, I'm okay with that.*

Just don't keel over before he gets here, Red Bathing Suit Woman said. *I want to see the show.*

Theo entered the stage from the same set of stairs we used. Yet another reason to almost die. The spotlight highlighted each of his curls. He wore his typical black leather jacket, red T-shirt, and jeans—but they looked anything but typical on him. His acoustic guitar was slung over his shoulder.

Frazzled Guide, whose hair had given up being tamed and now flowed freely, brought him a stool. She shook so much, I thought she was going to faint at his feet. Not that I would be far behind. I couldn't seem to catch my breath. *So much for all that walking,* I thought. Violet Page handed him her microphone. The smile he gave her would have melted steel.

"Thank you," he said. He repeated it until the crowd

settled down. "I'm thrilled to be here today and to give some support to these beautiful ladies." He gestured in our direction.

"Oh my gosh he *pointed at me!*" screeched Ashley.

Why bother to correct her?

He strummed the opening to "Dreaming Without You," and soon almost everyone was singing the chorus: "When I'm lying there and sleeping I'm just sleeping, when I'm sleeping without you; when I try to lie there dreaming, I'm not dreaming 'cause it's not dreaming without you . . ." During "Last Night" he turned around and asked us to dance. Guides, contest, rules—forgotten. Theo asked, we danced. I even caught Frazzled Guide swinging her newly freed hair around.

When "Last Night" trailed to a close, he raised a hand to silence the screams and applause.

"Is there time for one more?" he asked Violet, as if she'd be able to say no. When she nodded, he continued. "This is a new one. Let me know if you like it."

I almost couldn't hear him over the squeals. It was another pop song, "Ruby Red Hair." Everyone got into the groove.

His songs ended too quickly. The audience, eager for him to keep going, kept chanting "The-o, The-o," but they stopped when he passed his guitar to a guide and held up his hands as if to say "No more." Violet took the microphone and held her cheek out for a kiss. He obliged.

"Thanks, Theo. What a great performance! Now it's time to crown Miss HuskyPeach. Just a reminder, our winner receives not only the HuskyPeach tiara, but a five-thousand-dollar college scholarship, and a meeting with a modeling agency." The applause increased again.

How can she speak after Theo kissed her? I wondered.

"But before we crown her, we have prizes for two other contestants. Today's second runner-up, who displayed not only poise and beauty, but Grace Under Fire, will receive a two-hundred-fifty-dollar HuskyPeach shopping spree and be featured in our summer catalog shoot. Let's congratulate our winner, Miss Celeste Harris!"

I didn't move. *Me? I won something? A mistake,* I decided. I stayed still.

"That's you," Ashley hissed. She shoved me toward a smiling Violet, who held a bouquet of—*of course*—peach roses. From the audience, I heard hoots of "Celeste! Yeah!" My feet carried me to Violet. I took the flowers and she hugged me.

"Stand next to Theo," she whispered in my ear.

I heard her wrong. I had to have. "Stand next to *Theo*," she said louder, and nudged me in his direction. Confused, I walked to that side of the stage. And I would have fallen right off the side into the audience if he hadn't grabbed my hand.

Let's relive: *Theo Christmas took my hand!*

I have no idea who was first runner-up. I had no idea what my name was while standing next to Theo. I'd find myself staring at his profile, then I'd jerk my eyes to the audience, then a second later I'd be staring at him again.

At some point, Violet announced Miss HuskyPeach. This captured my attention enough for me to tear my eyes from Theo, who, truth be told, shot a couple of uncomfortable glances in my direction. I think the Monstrosity frightened him.

"Miss HuskyPeach—the face of our new catalog—is Miss Rosalie Fieldhart," Violet announced.

Who? I thought. I scanned the lines of girls behind me. *Frazzled Guide was looking for her earlier,* I remembered. But I didn't know who she was then either.

Curly blond-haired Bay-be stepped out from our group's line.

That's *her name!* I thought.

Then it was over. Violet thanked everyone for coming, said some other stuff about the pageant that I didn't pay attention to (still locked on to Theo Christmas), and dismissed the contestants. When Violet told us we could leave, I blinked and Theo was gone.

Was he really here? I thought as I hugged Ashley, Gail, and some of the other contestants. Gail and Ashley even promised to IM me and keep in touch post-pageant. Rosalie, whose personality lit up like neon when onstage, was back to her silent, floor-staring self.

Like a chandelier on a dimmer switch, Red Bathing Suit Woman commented.

Stop it! She just doesn't feel as good about herself offstage, I responded. I felt bad for her, because that's how I used to be.

Somehow, I navigated the crowd onstage without stabbing anyone with my roses and worked my way backstage. So many people swarmed the area that it was hard to find my parents. I spotted Violet Page, though, and wormed over to her.

"Hey Celeste, congratulations," she said. She hugged me. "You did great."

"Thanks," I said. "I just wanted to thank you for helping me out last time."

Violet turned pink. "Well, if I'd had stronger tape, maybe I would have been better help. I'm really sorry."

"Not your fault," I said. "Anyway—"

"Hey Vee!" A short guy, wearing a Giants cap and blue sweatshirt, launched himself at Violet and gave her a squeeze that would have made juice from an orange.

"Teddy!" she screeched. She pecked him on the cheek. "You were awesome today. I can't thank you enough for coming on short notice. The other guy cancelled at the last minute."

Not wanting to disrupt Violet's reunion, I inched away so I could make my escape and find Mom, Dad, and Ben.

"Celeste, wait." Violet stopped me with a hand on my arm. "I want you to meet my friend Teddy." Something about the way she said "friend" made me think "more than friends," if you get me. Same with the way she was looking at him.

"I think we've met. Kind of." He pushed his baseball hat back and winked.

Theo Christmas.

"You—you're friends?" I croaked. Couldn't breathe again.

"Shhhh," Violet whispered. "Don't tell. We try to keep private stuff private. Celeste has had a tough go of it lately," she said to Theo, "partially because of me. Be a sweetie and give her an autograph."

Instead of letting Christian move in with us, I wonder if Mom would adopt Violet.

239

"Why am I not surprised that you're causing trouble?" he teased. "Okay. I have a pen. Where should I sign?" He pulled a black permanent marker from the back pocket of his jeans.

I stood there, dumbfounded. I had nothing for him to autograph! The roses were wrapped in plastic, I didn't have any paper on me, Violet wasn't carrying her notes (like she ever did), and he didn't have anything either. The only thing I owned was—

"The dress," I said. "Sign my dress. It's the bridesmaid dress I'm wearing in my cousin's wedding this afternoon," I explained, when Violet looked horrified. "That's why it wasn't in your notes. The one I was supposed to wear ripped."

"You *have* had a tough time," Theo said. "Turn around. I'll sign the back."

Violet lifted the lace overlay, and I felt the marker dance across my back. Theo finished signing, then Violet gave me another hug and sent me on my way before I could process what happened. Later I would marvel at how swiftly the Monstrosity went from hated uniform to rescue outfit to The Most Treasured Item of Clothing I Will Ever Own for the Rest of My Life.

I wandered around backstage in a stupor until Ben found me for the second time that day. "She's over here," he called. I expected to see Mom and Dad, but my second shock (although not nearly as big, cute, or famous as Theo Christmas) came when I saw Katy and Millie, toting a big purse, behind him. The girls gave me a hug.

"Congratulations!" they squealed. "You didn't win!" I laughed with them.

Mom and Dad hugged me too, and told me how proud they were that I stuck with it. I gave Ben a high five for being my Wardrobe Expert.

"But why are you wearing your bridesmaid dress?" Mom asked.

"I'll tell you on the ride to the wedding," I said. "It's kind of a long story."

Millie and Katy said their good-byes. "We need to find my mom," Millie said, tugging on the string of the blue hoodie she was wearing and adjusting her bag. "I want to do some shopping before we leave. You're not the only one with stories."

I glanced from Millie to Katy.

"Mike called. Last night," Katy said.

"No way!" I squealed, and hugged them both.

"Maybe you and Alan can eat lunch with us sometime," Millie said, teasing. I blushed.

"Wait until I tell you what happened," I said to distract them. "I can't believe it."

"I can't believe that *dress*," Katy said. She wrinkled her nose. "It's hideous."

"It's beautiful," I said, and showed them Theo's signature. I heard a familiar "yip-yip!" over our latest round of squeals.

"Is that . . . ?" I began.

A wet brown nose popped out of Millie's purse.

"We couldn't leave him home," she said. "We'd never

make it back in time to . . . you know." She tried to push him back into the bag, but now that he had the spotlight, Couscous didn't want to give it up. He batted his big eyes and wagged his teeny tail at everyone passing by.

"Cute puppy." Violet, walking by, stopped to scratch behind his ears. "But does he look kind of . . . bloated to you?"

Millie checked her watch. "Uhh, can you show me where the ladies' room is?"

Katy giggled and they followed Violet into the mall.

Mom and I retrieved my clothes from the HuskyPeach dressing room. I tried to locate Elsa to tell her about the red dress, but couldn't find her. I'd have Mom call on Monday. They'd discover it soon enough, anyway.

On the ride down to Los Alvios, I told Mom about Christian's shoulder, Frazzled Guide and the Red Dress, and Super Ben's Wardrobe Swap. She just shook her head.

"It all came together, though," I said.

"It did. You look beautiful, even in that dress," she said. I gawked at her. "Don't tell your cousin, but it's the most awful thing I've ever seen."

We arrived at the church ten minutes before the ceremony was supposed to start. The bridesmaids were lined up outside like a row of peach parfaits, ready to proceed in.

"Do you remember what you're supposed to do?" Mom asked, smoothing some stray hairs in the mirror.

"Uh-huh," I said. I opened the door to climb out.

"Oh no, honey," Mom said. "There's a big black mark on

the back of your dress, under the lace. Aunt Doreen will flip if she sees it. Hold still and let me try to wipe it off."

"Sorry," I said, scooting out from under her hand and into the parking lot. "I earned that black mark." I blew her a kiss and jogged over to the other bridesmaids.

"How'd it go?" Kirsten asked. She hugged me, then handed me the day's second bouquet of flowers. Peach and white this time.

"Amazing," I said. "Tell you about it later."

And when you do, even Barbie Bridesmaid is going to wish she'd been a HuskyPeach today, Red Bathing Suit Woman murmured.

I smiled. Once again, she got it right.

Acknowledgments

Celeste would say that having your first book published is as exciting as not only *meeting* Theo Christmas, but having him show up at your house for dinner (hopefully Aunt Doreen won't be there to embarrass you). I'd say that it's ten million times that cool.

There are many, many people who helped me along the way. So I'd like to thank . . .

My parents, for their never-ending support, enthusiasm, and patience, and for always encouraging me to follow my dream. And for (sometimes) letting me get away with reading at the dinner table and with a flashlight under the covers.

My sister, Lindsay, for her support, joy, humor . . . and for a lifetime of good stories.

My grandmothers: Nina, for her love of laughter, and Mem, for her gift of words.

My agent, Sally Harding—personal cheerleader, voice of reason, and Champion of Celeste. You made my dream come true.

My Awesome Editor at Dial Books, Alisha Niehaus, for loving Celeste as much as I do and giving her story life. I could not have asked for a more talented, passionate partner in this endeavor. This book is a zillion times better because of your insight and skill.

My writer's group—Gary, Paul, Heather, Phoebe, Ruthbea, Sy, and Megan—who has been with Celeste from the beginning. Thank you for never letting me cut corners, pushing me to write better, and helping draft after draft after draft of this book take shape.

My cousin Susan, for providing the inspirational bridesmaid dress.

Dann Russo (dannrusso.com), for letting Theo Christmas sing his songs.

Wendy French and the Santa Barbara Writer's Conference, for encouraging me to take Celeste from short story to novel.

January Gill O'Neil, for being a wonderful friend, phenomenal poet, partner in literary endeavors, and inspirational Poet Mom.

The PEN/New England Children's Book Caucus, for choosing an early incarnation of *Models* as one of its 2006 Susan P. Bloom Discovery Night Award winners. And special thanks to Leslie Sills, who pulled Celeste from the pile, starting me on this journey.

The teachers who developed my love of reading and writing—especially Evelyn DeBaerstrand, Celia Baron, Pamela Painter, and Elizabeth Graver. And to Bonnie Rudner and Lisa Jahn-Clough, who rekindled my love of children's literature.

The friends and family who have cheered me on, including Dianne, Scott, Anne, Katie, Shelagh, Sarah, Kerri, Amy, J-Sav, Joe, and Ma and Dad C.

My husband, Frank, whose unwavering faith, love, and confidence in me gives me the freedom and courage to tell stories. I could never thank you enough.